WillowBrook Series

Book One

Mystic Tides

An Elemental Tale

Written by DC Daniel

Published by   ©Bookster Publishing LLC

7601 4th St N Ste. 300

St. Petersburg, Fl 33702

BooksterPublishing@gmail.com
ISBN: 978-1-965808-74-0 (softback)
ISBN: 978-1-965808-93-1 (hardback)
ISBN: 978-1-965808-73-3 (e-book)
Cover design and graphics created
by Bookster Publishing LLC
Printed in the United States of America
Second Edition, February 4, 2025

Digital Information

Author's Note: Transparency and Creative Process

As the author of the *WillowBrook* series, I want to assure all readers that every aspect and every element of the series—its intricate plots, unique theories, and rich character development—has been meticulously crafted by me without reliance on AI for conceptual creation. After the book was written, *Bookster Publishing* took over the editorial process to refine and polish the final manuscript.

The editing process was carried out by the skilled team at *Bookster Publishing Company*, with all corrections made by human editors to ensure the highest standards of publishing quality.

Visual Elements

The book's cover art and internal illustrations were created through a collaborative process involving both AI tools (specifically AI Genitor with Gencraft training) and Adobe Photoshop, and Canva, under the guidance of *Bookster Publishing* Company's design team.

Audio Transcriptions and Accessibility

All of book one's audio transcriptions should be available after 07/01/2025. Book one is currently in the funding process to have it narrated by human voice actors to deliver an authentic storytelling experience. For those who prefer to use AI-compatible reading devices or programs, that option is available at your choice as an epub reader. However, when funding is complete, and audio casting has been completed. Then you will be able to purchase directly through *Bookster Publishing*, human-narrated audio files are included as part of your order.

<u>Contact us</u>

If you have any questions or need assistance, feel free to reach out:

Email: BooksterPublishing@gmail.com

Order direct Website: www.WBSOME.com

Thank you for joining me on this magical journey through the WillowBrook series! Your support helps keep the magic of reading alive.

Sending Love, Light, and Magic

Preface

When I started writing the *WillowBrook* series, I had no idea how much it would change me. At first, it was just a way to gather my thoughts about growing as a person. But soon, it became a deep and personal journey, where I discovered struggles I'd faced, victories I'd won, and moments of clarity that shaped me.

I wasn't always great at reading, writing, or spelling when I was younger. Even though I earned a college degree in technology, I've still had to work hard to overcome feelings of not being good enough. But I kept going, determined to find a way to bring light and laughter to others.

One of the first authors who inspired me was Edward Packard with his *Choose Your Own Adventure* books. From there, I discovered other amazing writers like Dean Koontz and Stephen King. When I had kids, we enjoyed reading childhood favorites together, like J.K. Rowling's *Harry Potter*, R.L. Stine's *Goosebumps*, and Mary Pope Osborne's *Magic Tree House* series. These authors encouraged me to create my own stories filled with magic, mystery, and self-discovery.

This book isn't a guide to living a perfect life. Instead, it's a collection of stories, thoughts, and lessons I've learned along the way. Some are about my own life, while others come from the

  DC Daniel

people I've met and the experiences we've shared. My hope is that you'll see bits of your own story in these pages and maybe find a fresh way to look at your own journey.

I couldn't have done this without my friends and family, who cheered me on as I wrote. A huge thank-you to my editor for their amazing advice and for always believing in this book, even when I wasn't sure of myself.

And to you, the reader: thank you for taking this journey with me. Whether you're just starting out or have been on your path for a while, I hope this book gives you comfort, inspiration, or a sense of connection.

This journey isn't about reaching a destination—it's about growing along the way. I'm so grateful to share it with you. Sending you love, light, and blessings.

. ~ DC Daniel

BE BLESSED ~ ALWAYS BE KIND!

Table of Contents

Epilogue

Chapter Teaser: *The Magic of WillowBrook II*

❇ Dedication Page ❇

This first series has a special dedication, it goes to my very special very beary BFF 🐼 🫶 🐻 for being my cheer squad 📣, for never giving up on me, even when I gave up on myself. Also, a special dedication to my Harry Potter-believing Gen Z children (my little duckies 🐥 and my Gen Alpha Kiddos).

WillowBrook Motto

I am happy

I am healthy

I am radiant, I am bright

Filled with energy and passion

Shining like the morning light

I am beautiful

I am grateful

I am mindful

I am calm and stress-free

Embracing all the good around me

Living life in balanced harmony.

Become the Light Being

you are destin to be.

"Let your smile change the world, but don't let the world change your smile." ~DC Daniel

"Keep your head up, and keep swimming." ~DC Daniel

"Keep your Mana shining bright, and never stop believing in the power of your dreams and actions." ~DC Daniel

"Be extraordinary in the journey of life, because ExtraOrdinary people become Extraordinary Humans."

~DC Daniel

"My current situation is not my destination." ~DC Daniel

Chapter One

Mystic Tides

An Elemental Tale

Miss Juno always wanted children and is a guiding light of presence for her students in her school, trying to help them become their best selves.

Miss Juno is a woman in her late 30s with a warm and reassuring presence. She's sturdy and big-boned, and her face carries a unique, elongated charm.

Miss Juno's wavy brown hair frames her kind face, and her big green eyes are warm and comforting when she speaks. Though she couldn't have children, she stayed positive and understanding with the students she taught at school.

Over the past few years, Miss Juno saw Willow's struggles, but she always believed in her and the potential of all the kids she taught.

In early January, Miss Juno approaches Willow at the end of class. "Willow, will you stay after class? I need to talk to you?"

Willow responded with her cheery and upbeat demeanor. "Sure Miss Juno."

Miss Juno sits next to Willow, gently holding her hand and speaking softly. "I've been thinking, Willow. You're such a sweet, kind girl. I'd like to be your full-time guardian, if you'll have me."

Willow's face lights up with a big smile. She jumps out of her seat, almost knocking over her desk. "Yes, Ma'am! I'd be honored!"

Willow begins to become emotional and cry, the teacher opens her arms and hugs her. "You are a beautiful young lady, a gem in the rough. I'm so happy you said yes. I've always wanted a daughter."

They hug tightly, and Miss Juno kisses the top of Willow's head. "I'll call your social worker and get everything set up soon."

As Willow leaves for the bus, she waves to her soon-to-be guardian.

Her face glowing with happiness. Sitting on the bus, she thinks, *"My life is going to change, and it's going to be so much better now."* Feeling on top of cloud nine, she had no worries that, she was temporarily returning to the awful group home.

Soon, Willow was allowed to go and stay with Miss Juno. Initially, Willow is shy and reserved when she arrives at her new home. A few days into her new life, she settles into a routine, and her thoughts often wander off; *I am so happy to finally have my own guardian and a place to call home.*

Willow's future is looking really bright and full of hope, way more than she ever thought possible. She now lives at 1212 Sunset Drive in the Lake Nona area with her new guardian. Her new home is a big upgrade from where she lived before.

Juno's favorite saying is,

"Our home is a no-judgment zone.

Be yourself. ~ Love yourself.

You are always stronger than you think.**"**

Willow deeply values Clara's routine, which has become an essential part of Willow's daily life. Clara is a teacher at Willow's Middle School, she was not her teacher, but they still share a special connection.

Each morning, Willow would wake up early to ride to school with Juno, starting the day together. After school, Juno provides a safe, welcoming space for Willow, where she could finish her homework and enjoy a snack while Miss Juno graded papers and prepared for her classes.

In the evenings, they would sit at the dinner table, talking about their day while savoring a homemade meal.

One of their favorite traditions was playing a game during dinner, "Best Part and Worst Part of the Day," where they shared the highlights and challenges, they faced during their day. This nightly ritual brought them closer and created a comforting routine. For Willow, knowing that each day followed this familiar structure offered her immense comfort and peace.

Chapter Two

Meeting by Chance,

Friendships of a Lifetime

A few weeks later at lunch, a new girl approaches Willow at her table in the cafeteria, Kalei sits down next to her.

"Hello. new girl here. Kalei Applegate is the name, Lei Lei for short. What's yours?"

"My name is Willow, just plain Jane Willow."

Willow reaches out to shake her hand. "Nice to meet you." Kalei grabs Willow's hand and spontaneously pulls her closer to her, giving her an embracive **pūliki.** *(hug)*

Kalie says, **"Aloha_**Willow, nice to meet you.".

"Kalei, you have the most beautiful black hair I have ever seen, and your skin looks like it's been kissed by the sun. You're so lucky, I look like a blonde version of Casper the Ghost."

"Thanks, Willow…. My mom says it's because we are Polynesian that we have an out-of-this-world glow… I just finished enrolling, and they gave me my schedule, sent me to lunch, and told me to go make some friends."

Kalei chuckles. "Ha Ha Ha…I am like, yeah! it sooooo darn easy… to make friends when you're from a different land. You know, Willow, it's not the same here in Florida; it doesn't feel like the `*ohana*, I have on my island in Hawaii."

"Ohhh, what's `Ohana?"

"Well, it's a Hawaiian name for family."

"Kalei, your name is new to me; what's its meaning?"

"My 'ohana told me once that my name Kalei means the beloved child' or 'beautiful flower."

"Wow! Kalei, that sounds powerful."

Willow starts feeling inadequate compared to her new friend's name. She purses her lips, recalling past insults from the group home kids.

Overwhelmed with jealousy, Willow sardonically replies, "I wish I had a beautiful name like that.

No, I have Willow... like Weeping Willow... Ugg, I hate my life," with a shameful frown.

Kalei puts her arm over Willow's shoulder, offering comforting words, "You know, Willow, you shouldn't feel any way about your name. I think it's beautiful. Willow has a ring to it. I'm sure you were named Willow because you're strong and resilient."

Willow leaves behind the cloud of self-doubt and begins to smile, realizing she has a new friend. "Kalei, did they give you a schedule?" Kalei pulls it from her back pocket.

Willow looks over it, "OMG… This is happy dance time... this is so lit, can you believe it? We have a few classes together. I can show you around if you'd like."

Kalei responds excitedly, "That would be great... I feel lost; my school was only half this size, this school is huge…"

Through talking both girls discovered they had much in common from liking DreamWorks movies to other activities like skating and bowling.

They even enjoy similar foods and games on the internet, such as watching YouTube Reels, and Instagram feeds, they love to play RuneScape, and Fortnight.

After school, they meet up at the car loop.

"Hey, Kalei, what's your number? I'll text you later."

"Okay, let's swap phones. You put your number in mine, and I'll do the same."

They enter their numbers into each other's phones. Kalei hugs Willow and runs off to her dad's car.

Mr. Applegate honks the horn as Kalei leans out the window, shouting, "I'll call after dinner!"

They exchange waves. Willow smiles, feeling happy and excited about making a new friend.

Willows's inner thoughts ramble on in her head, as she walks over to Miss Juno's room. " *Like... OMG... how did I end up with this super caring and extraordinary lady? I started off as a sort of reject left at the hospital, unwanted and bullied my whole life. But hey, I'm rolling with it. She makes me feel all loved and full of the family vibes.* "

Over the next few weeks, Willow and Kalei become best friends. The girls start staying at each other's houses at least once a week.

Both girls' moms are thoughtful, caring, and incredibly loving. Kalei's dad is a riot!

His sense of humor is unmatched, and he often captures his goofy antics to share on Instagram and TikTok.

Steven Applegate works as an engineer at a tech company in Altamonte Springs. When he relocated to Florida for his job, the family had to adapt to the move. His engineering career is quite demanding, but Willow quickly observes that when he's not working, he's a Hoot!

It's about a month before Willow's 13th birthday, and they were both staying at Willow's house that night.

Miss Juno brought some popcorn to the balcony and hands it to them. "Girls, look over there! Do you see that full moon?"

Willow leans into Kalei. "Hey, Kalei, when's your birthday...?"

"My birthday is on July 13th. I'll be turning 13 this year. I can't wait till I'm 16 to start driving!"

"Gee-whiz, isn't that a coinkydink? Mine's on the 13th, too, but in June. We'll both be 13 real soon!"

They sit silently, staring at the beautiful stars and gleaming moon.

"Willow…. what are your plans? Are you going to party or do something with your mom?"

"I don't know, Kalei, I have never had a birthday party, at least one I can remember."

"I have always dreamed of balloons and a cake with candles."

"What! Willow, what do ya mean? Your mom has never thrown you a birthday party?"

"Well, Kalei, I got adopted by Miss Juno a few months ago. I've been in foster care since I was born."

"Oh, I'm sorry. Not like sorry you got adopted, but like, it must've been tough being in foster care for so long."

"Hey, if it helps, I have been through some lousy life cards, too; my dad passed away when I was 8. It was really…. really hard for a while, dealing with the sadness and loneliness. Then, my mom met my amazing second dad, Steven. He's my stepdad, so fantastic with me and my younger brother."

Willow says, as her eyes drop a few tears. "I'm happy you have two parents who love you. Things are good now for me, too. It's been the happiest time of my life since she adopted me.

I'm feeling super blessed now. The tough parts of my life are old news, like water under the bridge."

I'm sure your birthday will be awesome," Kalei looks empathically at Willow with a smile.

"Thanks, Kalei; I'm wishing for a cake and some balloons and having Miss Juno and you as my bestie to celebrate. Maybe we can go skating."

Kalei responds with a big grin, "That sounds like a blast! I love skating."

Chapter Three

Aurora Finds Her Wixan

The following weekend, Juno approaches Willow.

"Willow, would you like to have your very own pet?"

"Yes, ma'am, a fish? A cat? A dog? What kind of pet?"

Whatever kind of pet you want, just not a horse or a barn animal." Juno says jokingly.

"OMG! Like… really…Like are you serious as a heart attack? yeah! I have always wanted a cat to care for." Willow hugs Miss Juno. "Miss Juno, I would love to look at the humane society. That's where all the unwanted pets go. Unfortunately, it's kind of like a pet group home, which I know all too well. LOL!"

"Miss Juno chuckles. "Yes, dear, of course; that would be one way to look at it."

They went to the local Humane Society on a Saturday but couldn't find the right match. The two of them decide to venture over to the next town. Willow found herself head over heels for this breathtaking black cat with a peculiar mark on its forehead.

This cat has a perfect M shape etched right there like it was wearing a fancy feline crown.

And those eyes—oh boy, they were like twin golden lasers, piercing through Willow's soul. She was stunning, a cat queen ruling the kingdom.

This black cat has a cool and mysterious vibe, with a special M-outline mark on its forehead. Its fur is shiny and smooth.

The cat walks with confidence, like a lynx striding through the woods. The cat stands tall and proud in front of the glass, showing off its quiet strength and grace.

"Miss Juno, can I see that kitty…. that one, the black cat." She points to the gleaming big golden-eyed cat. Willow is over-excited and jumps up and down tugging at Juno's arm. "Do you see that one? It's at the end of the hall, staring right at us."

Judy, the pet caretaker, speaks up to them. "I don't think you want that cat…. That's a scratcher, and it's not people-friendly at all.

She was found abandoned in a taped-up box on the side of the road, resulting in its timid and mistrusting demeanor toward humans."

Despite the warnings, Willow insisted. "Judy, please, can I still see her, …. Pretty Please?

"Okay, if it's okay with your mom."

Clara said jokingly. "Sure, just be careful. We don't want you to get bitten. ….or get cat scratch fever." NO Turning into a cat woman at midnight!.

"Ha Ha, like that's really... a thing."

The cat paces back and forth, rubbing against the glass. When Willow comes into the room, the cat instantly connects with her. It jumps right up in her lap, rubbing itself on her and giving a deep, Purr of satisfaction. The cat begins to make biscuits on Willow's thigh. They communicate with each other as if they were old familiar friends.

"I just love the heck out of her, Miss Juno; can we please adopt her? Please…. pretty please with sugar on top…I can help you know, I will get a part-time job delivering papers or babysitting to help care for her."

"I appreciate your efforts to raise the cat; getting a job is unnecessary. Dearest Willow child, this is my gift to you. Just be good and do good in school okay?"

"Yes Maam… I promise to...always do my best." She raises her three fingers in the scout's honor.

With a keen sense of urgency, Willow was adamant that this was her forever pet. Miss Juno adopts the cat, and the three of them head home to start their new life together.

On the way home Willow sits in the car, gazing out the window.

She thinks to herself, *"This is so amazing, I now have my very own cat. It's a dream come true—someone to talk to, love, and care for."*

After arriving at the house, Juno gives instructions. "Willow, you must pick a name for Miss Kitty."

" Yes Maam, I will get to it straight away; I should have a name by dinner."

Willow gets deep in thought about this new name for the cat, she heads up to her room with the cat in her arms and shows it around. Sitting on the balcony with the cat, Willow tries to produce a name that is special and meaningful, something true to the cat's identity.

However, the cat did not seem to show interest in any of the names she suggests, including Salena and Gabriella.

Willow looking perplexed, stares at the cat, "I have a better name for you; how about Sybil?"

Having had enough of Willow's questionable name suggestions, Miss Kitty hisses like a tiny, furry drama queen and bolts into her room, unleashing a symphony of distressing meows.

Drama level: cat-attitude

MEOW!   Meow!!!

Meow!   Meow!!!

Undeterred by her feline friend's theatrics, Willow keeps throwing out names like confetti at a New Year's Eve party.

"Lilith, maybe?" Willow is to be met with more disdain by the midnight-colored furball.

Baffled by the cat's pickiness, Willow takes a break from the name game, probably to spare Miss Kitty from having an identity crisis. Willow strolls into her room to grab homework, leaving the cat to ponder the mysteries of nomenclature.

Willow returns with a newfound determination, ready to tackle both her math and science papers on the balcony.

She says to herself, "Well, onward... Nothing says academic excellence like naming your cat while doing Geometry and Science."

As she dives into her science assignment about the energy that surrounds people, trees, and animals, a sudden realization hits her like a comet. She glances at the cat, muttering, "I know I'm probably messing with your vibes!"

The cat wasn't just a sleek, black furball with a fancy name—it was a creature of energy and cosmic forces.

Willow's thoughts race to an epiphany, reverberating through her mind and across the balcony:

Miss Kitty's destiny demands a name as majestic as the galaxies themselves. It's time to quash this cosmic identity crisis.

Willow sprints into the room, dramatically standing in front of Miss Kitty with her hands on her hips as if she is discovering the secrets of the universe.

"Okay, I got it; hold onto your whiskers, Miss Kitty! I've cracked the cat-naming code! Miss Kitty, brace yourself for the name of the century! Drumroll, please! Are you ready?"

Miss Kitty cries out a long "Meeeooooow."

"I will call you... wait for it... drum roll, please..."

"Rainbow Whisker Sparkle Paws!"

She expects applause, but all she gets is the stink-eye glare. That says, *"Really, human, are you kidding me. Who's going to take me seriously? Rainbow Whisker Sparkle Paws?"*

The cat continues to give Willow this judgmental stare, wondering to herself, *"Has she finally lost her marbles or eaten too much catnip?"*

"No, just kidding, Miss Kitty, I don't want people to make fun of you. So, I've been pondering your majestic aura, Miss Kitty, and I've got it! You're not just an ordinary black cat with a gray M imprinted on its forehead; in my eyes, you're a cosmic color explosion.

I see hues of blue, purple, and green glowing from your coat, like a cat-shaped rainbow! So, the real drumroll, please... I dub thee... wait for it...Lady Aurora! You know, after your mystical energy. I think you are like the Aurora Borealis! Your colors flow like the northern lights."

She leaps into the air with the agility of a circus performer, extending her claws as if she's auditioning for the big top!

Willow swiftly evades her playful attack, moving with the grace of a ninja to avoid her enthusiastic clawing. Aurora lands gracefully on all fours, her playful energy still evident.

The room morphs into a feline fiesta, with Aurora launching into full-on kitty affection mode. She rubs against Willow's feet as if Willow has unlocked secret cat powers. Feeling like the feline chosen one,

Willow scoops her up, and in an instant, they're dancing as if they've stumbled upon a cat disco—complete with twirls and all.

Willow's happiness emanates, with Aurora's purring. It's like a tiny engine revved up to maximum volume, a symphony.

The cat, content with Willow's affection, expresses her love by rubbing her face against Willow's hand and delicately licking her thumb.

After a few minutes of dancing with Aurora, Willow hurries downstairs to find Miss Juno.

 As she leans in to speak to her, unaware of her excitement, she blurts out... "Hey, Mom."

Miss Juno replies without missing a beat with her new title. "Yes Daughter"

"I am sorry. I didn't mean to call you Mom. Perhaps it's too soon."

"It's okay honey. I would be honored if you called me Mom. Of course, only if you're comfortable with it."

Chapter Four

The Enigmatic Signs

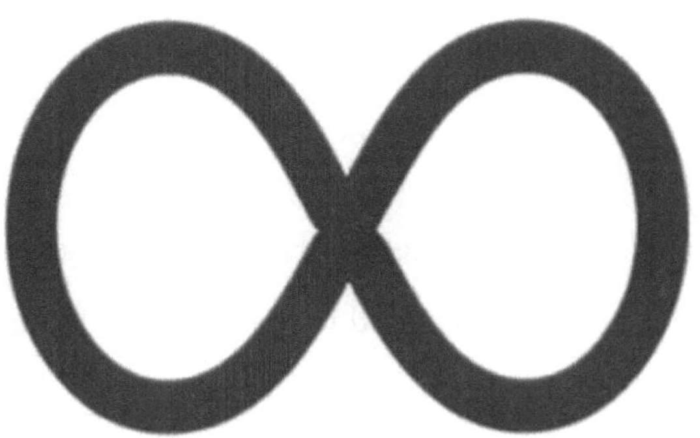

Willow's heart swelled with emotion as she tried to find the words. Tears filled her eyes, and she stumbled over her response between sobs of joy.

"YES Ma'am! Of course, I would love to call you Mom."

Her mom reached out to Willow with open arms.

"Come here, my precious child. I love you with all my heart."

She hugged her as if, finally, Willow had found the family and acceptance she had been longing for.

Embracing the hug, she gazes down at the stove; the aroma of something like sweet basil, garlic, and herbs fills her nose. "What are you making for dinner, Mom?"

"Spaghetti and meatballs with garlic bread and salad."

"Yummy…. that's my fav!"

Curiously, her mother asks. "Have you found her a forever name? or have you decided to leave her with the name Miss Kitty?"

"Yes! Oh My Gosh!!! Yeah, like, that's what we came down here to tell you. We had an eureka moment just a few minutes ago."

"So, Mom, Miss Kitty, and I went through a plethora of names like Salena, Gabriella, and Sybil, but she did not like any of them. I suggested Lilith, but she hissed at me and ran away.

Later, I was reading about Aurora Borealis in my science book; it hit me. So, like, I went to Miss Kitty and proposed the name Lady Aurora."

"Ohh Willow that is lovely."

"She was so happy she almost attacked me, thinking I was a Velcro mat waiting to catch her mid-air.

She landed next to me and started purring loudly with happiness." They both give out a giggle at the cat antics.

"The name you have chosen is beautiful. Aurora is a fine… furry name for her."

Juno looks endearingly into Willow's eyes. Then wells up in a few tears of gratitude.

As Willow turns away, she graciously smiles at her mother.

"Well, Willow, dinner is about to be done. Please go and place Aurora on your bed and wash your hands. Let's get ready to set the table."

Willow hums her melody, smiles at her mother, and then goes into another brief Cat Disco with the cat, doing the dip, shake, and twist. Going up the stairs to her room. She quickly without drying her hands, runs downstairs and sets the table.

Willow zooms downstairs, her stomach growling like a troll guarding his treasure.

The delicious aroma wraps around her like a cloak.

"Alright, Mom! It smells so good! I'm famished, I feel like, I could eat an entire feast worthy of a hobbit, complete with lembas bread and a side of roast dragon!"

Miss Juno lightly laughs, with a gentle smile, "Willow child, you are too funny, here is your plate.

A steaming pile of spaghetti with three meatballs nestled next to a piece of garlic toast.

They both sit at the table to converse during dinner time.

"Would you like to say the prayer tonight, or would you like me to lead?"

"I'll say the prayer… because I have so much to be thankful for."

They reach for each other's hands and lower their heads, and Willow starts.

"Dear God, we have gathered to share a meal in your honor. Thank you for bringing us together as a family and thank you for this food. Please feed our souls with the bread of life and help us to do our part in kind words and loving deeds to others. Bless this food to our bodies, Lord. We thank you for all the gifts you've given to those around this table."

Together, Willow and her mother in unison say. "Amen."

"So… Willow, how was school?"

"I got an A on my math test and B minus on my vocabulary. Miss Schultz said I needed to study my vocab more, but other than that, my day was good. I gotta say, I am so over these masks, they are a total bummer. Half the time, you taste what you last had to eat. And the fact you can't breathe easily while your nose and mouth are covered… this really bites Narwhals."

"Yes, I understand your feelings; sometimes, it feels like I am suffocating. And you are so very right!" Having smoldering bad breath stinks in a mask.

We must keep swimming, we have to do, what we have to do,"

Her mother rolls her shoulders and then says, "The famous phrase…**c'est la vie!**.

My child... **c'est la vie!**…You're protecting yourself and others by wearing your mask."

"Well, on a happier note, the bullies from the foster care home haven't bothered me in the last week, which has tremendously reduced the stress in my life. Well, enough about me. How was your day, Mom?"

Her Mother sighs a little. "My day was challenging because of those new kids from Michigan.

They are a pair of unruly twin boys who always give me grief. I know they'll come around eventually like all the children do, but in the meantime. Good grief! What am I to do… but say c'est la vie!"

They finish their meal with their Best Part and their Worst Part of the Day, and small talk. Willow clears the table and heads to the kitchen to help her out with the dishes and tidy up. Just then, the doorbell rings.

"Mom! I'll get the door…"

Willow rushes to the door and opens it with excitement. "Hi Kalei…. Good evening, Mrs. Applegate, welcome."

In her pleasant and eager demeanor. "Come on in. Mom and I just finished up with dinner."

"That's great, Willow; I am glad we didn't interrupt. Is your mom busy? I popped in to talk to her for a few."

"She's in the kitchen through those white louver doors."

Willow looks at Kalei. "Let's go upstairs. I want to show you my new pet. Mom got me a cat today. Her name is Aurora."

Without haste, they hurry upstairs. Willow bends down in front of Aurora, rolling her hand over the top of the air over Aurora like she is introducing the Queen of England or something. "Kalei, meet Lady Aurora."

Kalei, in her joking manner, bends over and takes a bow. "My good Lady Aurora, it is a pleasure to meet you."

Funny enough, Aurora meows and bow's down to her front paws, like Kalei, just met the queen of a far, far away land, like a mystic ruling cat empress. The girls giggle at the cat's silly antics.

After a wee bit of time passes, they turn their focus on their class studies, due tomorrow.

Willow picks up her science book and homework while Kalei also gathers her homework papers.

She follows Willow to the balcony. They sit on the papasan chairs and complete their assignments.

Sometime later.

Willow, feeling a strange sensation, says. "Why does my hand feel so hot?"

Willow looked down and held out her hand. It was glowing with a restless pulse. She focuses on her hand, which continues to emit a faint, warm glow.

As she flexes her fingers, feeling the energy coursing through her veins. It was an odd sensation but not entirely unpleasant.

She holds her hand out towards the balcony.

Kalei's eyes widened in surprise. "Whoa."

Kalei leans in for a closer look. "What's going on? Did you bump into something hot?

Willow shakes her head. "No, nothing like that. It just started feeling hot and now it's glowing."

Kalei intently stares, studying Willow's hand.

"That's weird; I've never seen anything like it."

Willow nods, feeling a mix of curiosity and apprehension. Her thoughts race once again. *I wonder what this means… if anything.* Her thoughts went deeper, *"Am I developing some kind of superpower? Or is this just a fluke, something that will go away on its own?"*

Willow's thoughts respond, and her hand suddenly stops glowing. She flexes her fingers again, feeling the residual warmth slowly dissipating.

Kalei says, breaking the silence. "Well, that was interesting. Do you think it's some kind of magical thing?"

Willow shrugs. "Who knows? Science always has my interest and stuff like that, but I never really believe in magic or anything of that nature."

Kalei nods. "Yeah, me neither. But maybe there's more to the world than we thought."

Willow smiles. "Maybe you're right…. Who knows what kind of mysteries are out there, waiting for us to discover?"

With that, the two girls settle back into their chairs, watching the sun slowly dip below the horizon.

For Willow, the strange incident with her hand was just the beginning of a much larger journey that would take her to the limits of her imagination and beyond. She tries to focus on her science studies, but her mind keeps wandering, trying to make sense of the strange sensation she has experienced.

As the wind continues to pick up, Willow feels a sudden surge of energy coursing through her body.

It was like nothing she had ever felt before—a mix of excitement and fear that left her with labored breathing.

"OMG, Willow, are you okay?"

Aurora stands up, arches her back, and hisses, evil enough to stir the dark side, alerting them to something not inviting.

"Something is not right…"

"What' cha mean?"

I don't know, but everything looks super foggy and blurry."

"Should I get your mom?"

"Kalei, do you hear that humming? It's sort of a melody. It's getting louder and closer."

The cat is now making louder hissing noises and pacing across the balcony's edge.

"Okay, like seriously, you are freaking me out…. Are you sure you don't want me to get Miss Juno?"

Willow says with a strange look on her face. "Wow, that's weird and a little eerie.

Just like that, everything is quiet now. I only hear the crickets and bullfrogs."

Aurora still paces back and forth on the ledge. She is now crying in distress and acting unsettled.

As Willow stands up to console her cat, a giant bat three times the size of a normal bat comes flying into the side of Willow's head.

"Wack!"

The crazy bat attaches itself to her hair. Willow begins to scream as she twists and turns.

"Get it off of me!"

Aurora makes a matrix catt-a-tude move. She leaps off the ledge and does a 360-degree flip, landing on top of the bat, digging its claws deep into it.

As Aurora grabs the bat, she pushes off Willow's head and leaps back to the balcony ledge with a precise landing, bat in tow. Aurora shakes the bat repeatedly and flings it off the edge. The injured bat falls to its demise.

"Come on Willow, grab your stuff and the cat; I want to go in. This is totally freaking me out."

"Yeah, I am right there with you, it's like my cat went into Mr. Beast mode on that bat."

When Willow shuts the second French door behind her, a gust of wind whips her papers out of her hands. They go flying through the air in a whirlwind tunnel.

Willow is determined to take control. She marches, the door closed. They settle in her room with Aurora to finish their assignments.

The next day at school, everything appears normal and on schedule.

At lunch, the girls were rambling on about many things.

"Kalei, have you heard about the camping trip next month?"

Kalei answers, "I think I saw something in the 5th-period hall outside Mrs. Runkle's room.

"Kalei, that's right, I saw it posted there too. I overheard the assistant principal of the school talking about Operation Snowball Getaway.

They are organizing the camping trip for the weekend for all of us kids in the Snowball group. I have never been camping before."

Kalei squalled with excitement.

"Eeekkkk! It's been a quick minute since I have been camping."

Kalei was far more excited than Willow, eagerly rambling about what outfits to pack and wondering who we'd be sharing a cabin with. Their excitement was contagious, and it felt like they could hardly wait for the trip to begin.

Chapter Five
Discovery Camp

As the girls hop onto the bus, bags in tow, the two moms can't resist a bit of chit-chat.

They bid their daughters farewell with enthusiastic waves as the bus rumbles away from the school parking lot.

Casually, Sarah decides to break the ice. "By the way, Miss Juno, my name is Sarah Applegate. What's your first name?"

With a friendly grin, Miss Juno spills the beans. "Oh, you can call me Clara or just Juno. At school, I go with Miss Juno because, you know, we've got to keep our respect and order at school. It's nice to meet you!"

The moment seems ripe for a warm, friendly hug. Sarah leans in, wearing a grin that could light up a room, and whispers conspiratorially, "Juno, you know! The girls are on the brink of becoming little elemental prodigies. Willow and Kalei are gearing up for their Elemental Earth blessings on their 13th birthday!"

 Clara takes it all in stride, not hearing the hidden message. She responds with a chuckle, "Ah, yes!

They're growing faster than we can keep track of. blink, and they'll be 15 going on 30, navigating the mysterious world of teenage wisdom."

Clara laughs lightly and continues, "Please, Lord, give us the strength to endure the teenage years without locking them up and throwing away the key. Let's leave them in the fair Maidan's tower until they turn 30."

Sarah chuckles a little, then redirects Clara in whispers. "You know that's not what I am talking about… Willow is special, just like Lei Lei."

Miss Juno responds unknowingly. "I don't understand what you're saying."

Then Sarah goes into further detail.

"The girls will evolve here real soon, on their magical birthdays. You see, Willow is changing. She is growing stronger; I see it in her aura.

My daughter is going through the change too. With every full moon or new moon, it's bound to happen very soon."

Clara gasps as if someone had just stalled the air right out of her lungs.

Then, she responds with an innocent, unknowing parental demeanor, "What do you mean coming of age? How can you see someone's aura? What do you see happening in their near future?"

"I cannot tell you exactly, Clara, but what I do know is the girls are changing quickly. You know the girls will come of age and evolve into their higher selves. They won't be able to go to this middle school here."

    **DC Daniel**

"What in the green eggs and ham are you talking about? Where are they supposed to go to school?"

"They're both going to have to join the other magical kids at WillowBrook. The school for inspiring Wixan's. WillowBrook School of Magic is the best education and instructions a magic child can obtain."

"Magic School … yeah right…ah humbug. What April fool's joke are you playing here?"

"This is no joke, Clara. I am for real. The school is located between California and Hawaii on a secret cloaked island named Solaris. WillowBrook is a very safe Magic School, so you have nothing to worry about. I know it's a hard concept to grasp, but it's the truth, Clara. Just wait and see."

Just then, Clara's cell phone rings and she answers the call straight away. When she answers the call. "Sarah, pardon me, I must take this; I appreciate your point of view on the girls. I will catch up with you later." Mrs. Applegate nods and waves bye.

Meanwhile, as Willow leans forward toward Kalei on the bus…. "Selfie Time"

Kalei leans in with a smile. "Best Time Ever!" Kalei leans in front of Willow, mischievously reaching behind Willow, giving her bunny ears.

Willow throws up a peace sign. Both girls smile and snap the photo. Willow writes #BESTDAYEVER. #SPRINGSNOWBALL; in the corner.

The rest of the kids are taking selfies and singing road trip songs. All the kids participate by posting on social media on the way to the camp. They arrived at the camp later that morning. The group of kids are standing and waiting to get assigned to cabins, groups, and camp counselors.

Chapter Six

Campfire Whispers and Midnight Escapes

Mrs. Simmons announces. "Kalei, Willow, Zeda, Fran. I choose you four as cabin 9's, cabin mates."

The girls squeal with delight that they get to stay in the same cabin. They introduce themselves to each other and head off to cabin nine.

Upon arrival, counselor Simmons instructs them. "Alright, ladies, unpack and make your way to the Cove to collect a copy of the weekend's activities."

"Mrs. Simmons, do we have to wear our masks here?" asked Zada.

"Yes, child, we're still acting as a school function… and furthermore, you want to protect yourself and others.

So, unless you're swimming, everyone, please wear your mouth coverings."

All the girls give a long exasperation. "Ahh, really!"

As Kalei's group joins the other preteens at the camp, everyone gets a copy of the activity schedule.

The list outlines an exciting array of activities for the weekend, including canoeing, bow and arrow target practice, a scavenger hunt, campfires, and too many more activities to list.

The girls can hardly believe how much fun they'll have and are thrilled with the prospect of participating in all these activities.

This Friday night, a group of young girls and their new acquaintances thoroughly enjoy themselves, huddled together around a campfire. They share eerie ghost stories and engage in lively conversations while indulging in S'mores and delectable treats.

As the clock strikes 10:00 pm, the counselors rally the kids to make their way back to their cabins for the night.

Despite the late hour, the girls continue to chatter, primping their appearance and updating their social media accounts. Eventually, Zeda and Fran succumb to slumber, leaving Willow and Kalei to their own devices.

Counselor Simmons is also well on her way to a peaceful night's sleep. As the night wears on, the two adventurous young girls quietly slip out of their cabin, making their way through the shadowy forest to the tranquil shores of the Cove.

Chapter Seven

The Gift of the Elements

The new moon acts as their guide, illuminating the path and filling them with a sense of wonder. Undisturbed and utterly alone, the pair walk hand in hand towards the pier, their spirits still buoyant from the day's activities

Upon reaching the dock, they are met with a breathtaking sight the moon's reflection glistening on the water below, creating an ethereal, almost magical atmosphere that seems to emanate from the heavens. From their vantage point, they can even see the powerful waves crashing against the rocky outcroppings on the breaker bar to the opening of the ocean. The soothing sounds of crickets and frogs fill the night air, adding to the calm and serenity surrounding them.

The girls kick off their shoes and dangle their feet into the cool, refreshing water off the pier, giggling as they start splashing each other playfully.

Their childlike laughter echoes throughout the Cove. Bathed in the soft, shimmering light of the moon, the girls' hair seems to glow as they hold hands, creating a bond that feels unbreakable.

Willow turns to Kalei and makes a special request.

"Let's make a BFF Pact.

Repeat after me, we're the BFF team,
Best Friends Forever, living our dream!
We'll share our hopes and all our zest,
With you by my side, life's simply the best!

Through ups and downs, thick and thin, We'll laugh together, and always win. Friends till the end, through every endeavor, BFFs, forever and ever!

Kalei echoes her words, repeating the pledge sincerely and heartfeltly.

The girls clasp their pinkies, interlocking tightly, symbolizing the deep and everlasting friendship they have just formed. They are true best friends, committed to supporting and caring for each other, through thick and thin.

As the girls chat about their plans, Kalei can't help but notice something peculiar about Willow's hand. In the soft glow of the moonlight, a small crescent moon shape seems to be shining on the top of her hand.

Excitedly, Kalei draws Willow's attention to the glowing symbol, and Willow is taken aback, rubbing her hand in disbelief.

"Kalei, it's happening again, that weird sensation…the energy pulsing through my body. Everything is getting blurry again. You see the fog rolling in … don't you?"

"Yes, Willow this time I see it. I hear a melody off in the distance, too."

"Yeah, this is the same thing that happened at home on the balcony."

The symbol quickly vanishes, leaving the girls feeling bewildered and confused. Hastily, they return to their cabin, their steps quick and urgent. Suddenly, they both stop in their tracks, a silent understanding passing between them. *"What just happened?"*

They cry out in unison, talking over each other in confusion. After a moment of chaos, Willow holds up her hand, with the top of her hand facing Kalei, and urges her to speak first. Kalei hesitates for a moment, then blurts out, "I saw it too— the crescent moon on your hand. I've never seen anything like it."

"The melody is getting louder, Kalei."

"I hear it; look over there. There's a rustling in the woods."

"What should we do? Should we hide?"

This lady with long, silver hair appears out of the fog; she is adorned in a flowing black and purple robe trimmed with the golden embossed tree of life symbols at the top of the lapel as energy pulses through the trim of her robe.

"No, my young enchantress's. It's okay, I am a friend. Don't be scared."

"My name is Gabriella. I am one of the forest keepers. Willow and Kalei, you are some of the special ones. You will receive a special gift on your 13th birthday."

As she speaks these words, the air around them begins to shimmer and glow with a soft, ethereal light.

The rustling in the woods grows louder and more insistent, as though the very trees themselves are whispering secrets to the children. Suddenly, a gust of wind sweeps through the clearing, carrying the sweet scent of blooming plumerias.

"This gift is something that will allow you to harness the power of your elemental nature. You must use this gift wisely, for with great power comes great responsibility."

Willow inquires. "What great power… what are you talking about?

"I think I know Willow. My **tūtū** told me something about my 13th birthday a long time ago."

"Mrs. Gabriella, do we get to go learn magic, capture a dragon, and fight off evil spirits?"

"Willow and Kalei, my children, always remember to keep the balance in nature and never misuse the gifts you have. Dark forces in Spector's shadows are trying to gather lost souls and create an evil army to add to Hades Underworld to ruin everything good. But don't worry young ones; I'm here to guide and protect you. I used to be part of the Order of the 12 Elements, but now I'm retired.

We're all connected, like the magic in the ancient forest around us, part of the universe as one."

She gently blows on the globe, and it disappears into golden sparkle dust, which covers them with a golden glowing light.

"Both go forward with the magic and knowledge to keep your Mana strong."

"Look! Willow, we are glowing and shining bright like diamonds." As Kalei twirls around, with glowing dust trailing her.

"Yeah, this is so totally cool," Willow exclaims with a wide grin. She effortlessly executes a backflip, landing it flawlessly, and leaves a dazzling trail of glowing dust behind her, showcasing her gymnastic prowess.

"Soon, you two should receive a special puddle-hopping delivery. We are watching and waiting for you, my young ones."

With the flick of her wrist, she says.

"Departure No low Aires"

And like magic, the lady disappears into thin air.

With disbelief on Kalei's face, she says. "A puddle hopping delivery. I think that lady goes koo koo for coco puffs. How would a puddle hop and deliver anything not soaking wet?"

"I don't know Kalei. This is all too much to take in; look, my hand is returning to normal."

"Yeah, I see, I think we should call it a night. It's like three in the morning. Our Netflix mystery needs a rest."

"I agree. Maybe this is a dream, and when we wake, this will never have happened."

The girls exchange a knowing look and continue their way, the mystery of the glowing symbol, the lady, and her words, still fresh in their minds. They get to their cabin, then settle in, changing into their pajamas before climbing onto their respective bunks.

Willow lays there, her mind racing with questions about what just happened.

Chapter Eight

A Golden Glow in the Night

Meanwhile, Kalei is equally mystified by the strange occurrence. Suddenly, she feels a warm sensation on the back of her hand.

Kalei kicks Willow's top bunk.

"Hey, are you awake?

"I am now, what's up?"

"Look at my hand. Now mine is glowing. It looks like an upside-down triangle."

Willow climbs down off the bunk bed. She stands there stunned and quickly gets out her phone to snap a picture.

One of the photos comes out blurry, while the others are nothing more than a bright purple light coming from her hand.

"I can't get a good picture. Rub it, lets see if it disappears, like mine did."

Kalei rubs it, it fades away.

As they lay there, the image of the glowing hand and the triangle pattern on Kalei's hand keep replaying in their minds.

They can't sleep, they feel restless and anxious, unsure of what to make of the strange occurrences. The girls decide to sit on the front porch of the cabin.

Both of them spend some time trying to figure out what happened as they discuss their thoughts and theories.

"Hey Kalei, I've got this wild theory – what if we are part of a secret society of supernatural powers, like those characters in movies?"

"Tish! Tish! Kalei, I highly doubt it, but I can't deny that lately, life has been a bit too Netflix and not enough chill."

"Let's put our potential powers to the test! Open up X, the new search engine on your phone."

"Uh-oh, my internet is on a coffee break. I've got zero bars – not even a snack bar!"

"Join the club! I'm in the 'No Bars Anonymous' too.

Maybe our supernatural abilities are on strike, demanding better working conditions. Guess they're not fans of the new search engine X either!"

"You said your **tūtū** told you about these things, right?"

"Yeah, a little about nothing…She never said it was like we would be invited to a melodic concert, that no one gave us tickets to!

Just when they think, they are in for the ultimate show, poof! Everything goes silent. Total quiet. Pin-drop silence. But then, surprise, surprise! There is some more rustling in the bushes to the left of them.

They spin around, and guess who strolls out from the woods? None other than the same old lady with the long, silver hair and ocean blue eyes, that could probably see through walls.

This time, though, she isn't empty-handed. Nope. She has a trident staff, like she just finished a shift in the mystical weapon department.

And oh boy, she is rocking the same purple and black flowing cloak, but this one is like the deluxe edition. It has different symbols pulsing on and off in beams of light, six on each side.

"Wow Kalei, she changed it up, talk about fashion with a side of magic!

Kalei is like, "Whoa, hold up, what's happening here? I feel like a magnet being pulled towards her."

They grab each other's hands.

"Willow what in the flying monkeys is going on?"

"I don't know but we are floating towards her."

They arrive in front of her, still holding hands in shock and disbelief.

Willow speaks up, "Okay, Gabriella you mysterious lady, spill the magic beans!"

The old woman speaks in a soft, yet commanding voice.

"I came back to give you an important message that I forgot before. The order has been waiting for you. You've been chosen to continue the legacy of the ancient ones."

The girls are confused but intrigued. The old woman continues, as she touches Kalei and Willow's hands. Their hands start to illuminate.

"You see Kalei, the symbol on your hand, my child, is the mark of the water goddess. You have been chosen to be one of the water emissaries in this world."

This upside triangle proceeds to pulsate as Gabriella directs her attention to Willow.

"My child you are special too, as I told you before, the mark on your hand is because you have been chosen to have special elemental values of the moon goddess."

"You too are in favor of the Hypogeum

ancient ancestors, the great ones."

The girls hang on to every word she says. They have never heard anything like this before. The elder woman explains further holding a glowing ball.

Secretly murmuring in that mystical tone, Gabriella spills the cosmic tea:

"Young Ladies' get ready as, Earth's magical sidekicks, because this is just the beginning of your wild and whimsical adventure!"

She gently blows on the globe, as she holds on to it and it disappears into sparkling golden dust, that covers their hair with a golden glowing light."

"Both of you go forward with the magic and knowledge to keep your Mana strong."

"Look! Willow, we are glowing and shining again."

With the flick of her wrist, she says.

"Departure No low Aires"

And like magic, the lady disappears into thin air.

"I don't know Kalei; this is all too much to take in. Look my hand is returning to normal."

"Mine too, Willow."

"I think we should call it a night. It's now like four in the morning."

Chapter Nine

Mystical Encounters & Unveiling Hidden Powers

The following day, the girls wake up groggy from their late-night adventure. They grab their meditation mats, comb their hair quickly.

After splashing their faces with chilly water in the showers, feeling revived and awake, they go down to the Cove. They arrive and see that most other campers have already, set up their mats in a circle. The girls join them, taking their places in the group like during their snowball meets at school.

The group recites their snowball motto together in unison, as the Bette Midler's song. "Wind Beneath My Wings" plays in the background."

"Do my best, strive for success, raise each other up, and stay true to myself and aware of my actions. We are all unique, original, and show self-love."

The group continues with five self-care rules. Everyone sounds off, in unison.

"1.) I promise always to love myself enough to be myself. I am smart, bright and happy."

"2.) I practice abstinence from sex, drugs, alcohol, and anything else that can be addicting to my life.

"3.) I love myself; I am in control of what happens to me; I am the creator of my destiny."

"4.) For I am, Everything, I do, I say, I act and think."

"5.) ALWAYS DO GOOD~ ALWAYS BE KIND!!!"

Miss Shoemaker takes charge and guides them into a state of relaxation. Soon, they all hum the mantra of the day, surrendering to the present moment.

As time passes, Willow and Kalei experience an ethereal sensation, feeling light as air. Suddenly, their energy elevates, and they hover 2ft above their mats. With a curious gaze, they look at each other and down at their bodies, awestruck by the sight.

However, the moment is fleeting. With a jolt of energy, they swiftly return to their physical selves and land on their mat.

"Thud!"   " Kur plunk!"

Willow and Kalei open their eyes, they exchange a look of wonder and disbelief. They notice three fellow campers staring at them with confusion and amazement.

The girls quickly exchange glances before shutting their eyes again, pretending not to have seen the others' gaze. However, their minds are racing, and they cannot return to their meditative state.

As the session ends, Willow keeps a watchful eye on the behavior of the three other campers, hoping to gauge whether they behold witness to the experience.

The two boys next to them, remain still and unaffected. When Kalei makes eye contact with the other girl in the group, she seems to be staring back at them.

After class, she approaches the duo with a friendly smile. In a state of suspense, neither Willow nor Kalei speak, waiting for the girl to break the silence. "Hello, you two."

She is a little taller than the two girls, with defining emerald, green eyes. The new girl is wearing a braided crown with the rest of her long jet-black hair flowing in the gentle breeze.

This girl reaches out her hand, "Hi, I am Trinity."

The two friends exchange glances before shaking her hand and introducing themselves.

"Hi, I am Willow, and this is Kalei."

Kalei pipes in. "Trinity, it's nice to meet you."

"Do you two want to join me for lunch?"

Kalei responds happily. "Sure, sounds great; I hear we're havin' coconut shrimp and salad today."

Trinity points towards the girls' cabins, "I'm right over there in cabin eight."

"That's so lit Trinity, we, are right beside you, we`r in cabin nine." Willow puts a high five in the air and meets trinity's hand in mid-air.

Chapter Ten

Whispers of Magic and Danger

They make their way to cabin nine first. At the same time, Kalei puts up her yoga mat.

Willow inquires. "Trinity, did you see anything peculiar during morning meditation?"

Kalei turns and gleams at her as her mouth gapes open, and a ghostly shock comes over her, looking too white to be a ghost.

Kalei, going straight poker face, chimes in. "No other than that kid Timmy and his stinky feet… The girls laugh as Kalei elbows Willow in the side in a low, grumbling voice. "What are you trying to do… get some witches, stoned?"

Trinity overhears Kalei's remark and feels her need to share her plethora of knowledge. "You know, you two, my great Aunt was stoned for believing in something other than Christianity. So, I have heard many folktales from my parents.

The burning of the witches of Salem, these terrible things happened, you know, witches getting stoned to death or burned alive at the stake." She shakes her head, looking at the ground., and then looks back at them.

"Not good, my friends… not good at all…. So please, let's not talk about such Witches' demise of the past."

Both girls nod in agreement. For the better part of the morning, the three girls spend time together, making memories and participating in camp activities.

Later that day, under the cover of darkness, Kalei and Willow retrieve their phones and head down to the Cove, arriving at the same dock as the previous night.

As they ponder the cause of their mystical experiences, they need help to produce satisfactory explanations of what they might be able to do with their powers.

They begin to surf the web on the X platform, finding nothing to support their encounters.

However, Kalei suddenly remembers a folktale from her **tūtū**. "You know… now we have time to talk, Willow.

My Tutu tells me this: according to the story, there are children in this world who are born with a special mark, signifying that they have a unique connection to the elements of the earth."

"Lei Lei, stop joshing me… let's be serious."

"Will, I am being straight up with you." Kalei finishes sharing this story with Willow, who grabs her by the shoulders and looks at her wonderingly.

"Could we be the ones with this special mark?"

"I don't know, Willow, but I hope my **tūtū** is right. I think I could kick arus at being a magical one."

Overwhelmed by the possibility, Willow is left speechless as she processes this latest information.

The girls collect pebbles from the dock and skip them across the water, enjoying the moonlight and chatting about their new friend Trinity, their family back home, and how this has been the best trip ever. As the night wears on, they become aware of the approaching witching hour and realize it's getting late. Agreeing it's time to turn in, they quietly return to their cabin, change into their nightclothes, and settle into their beds for a peaceful night's rest.

The following day, the girls wake up to excited chatter among their cabin mates and the girls from Cabin Seven.

They discuss the various activities planned for the final day at camp. Some consider the zip line and ropes course, while others lean towards the horseback riding adventure.

Willow and Kalei are eager to participate in the day's activities, and they discuss their options.

Just then, Trinity asks, "Are you ready for an adventure?" The girls exchange their thoughts and preferences, with Willow expressing her fear of heights.

"What about horseback riding, Trinity?" Kalei asks.

"Kalei, I am good with whatever you two want to do."

"YOLO ladies, let's overtake my fear of heights." Says Willow. Kalei reaches for a high-five and shouts. "You got this girl, what do you have to fear…… but fear itself."

Willow smiles eagerly. "Yes, let's make this a no-fear day.

Grinning ear to ear, Trinity says to the other girls, "Let's go on the zip line adventures and then Horseback riding…."

As the two girls walk ahead of Trinity, Trinity chats with her other cabin mates. They head towards the morning meditation with their yoga mats in hand.

"I don't want to go to meditation today," Willow tells Kalei.

"Yeah, me either; I feel anxious about what happened yesterday."

"You know, Kalei, if they find out we can levitate, we risk being ostracized by everyone."

Kalei says, "I can already hear the heckling. Everyone hide your black cats and brooms. I hear that Kalei is in search of a new one."

Willow chimes in. "Or Like….Oh, no! Look Out! For the evil witch! Prepare to be turned into a Leaping Lily Lizard! Watch out, folks! She will cast a spell on you."

"Willow, I am not going to fret about this; I think we will be fine; let's just amidst the haste and sit and pretend to meditate…I think we will be in the clear if we stay out of the meditation trance."

They grab each other's pinkies and interwound them, shaking their pinkies and confirming their secret pac.

The day unfolds without any notable incidents. The girls are acutely aware of their emotions and energy levels as they embark on their zip-lining escapades alongside Trinity. Following a thrilling morning, they visit the petting zoo barn and feed the animals some treats. In the afternoon, the trio convene with fellow campers at the pool for further activities.

Kalei confides in Willow that she has an inexplicable dread about herself.

She senses that something tragic is about to occur. Despite Willow's efforts to console her, Kalei's unease persists.

As the three girls play Marco Polo in the pool, they hear bloodcurdling screams from a distance.

Kalei looks down and spots a tiny lifeless body at the bottom of the 12 foot pool; without hesitation, with one big breath of air, Kalei dives to the bottom of the pool like a mermaid with her legs fused.

She scoops the child up and with two big mermaid tale flicks, she flies outta the water. Conveniently at the edge of the pool, with no harm or troubles, she lays the lifeless boy's body on the edge of the pool. His lips are blue and he is not breathing. The lifeguards rush over to perform CPR on the boy; soon, he expels the water and is fine.

The other campers are stunned and confused.

One of the counselors comes to take over the care of the revived kid and thanks the girls for their quick thinking and life-saving actions. Kalei and Willow quietly leave the pool, still processing what has happened. They share a deep connection, and their telepathic communication grows more robust over the weekend.

They look at each other without saying a word. The two of their minds meld in communication.

"You know, Kalei, everything's going to be OK!"

"Willow, we should keep this to ourselves until we get home."

Willow nods her head and acts out a key locking her mouth, not saying a word but just using telecommunication.

"I completely agree with you…. mum's the word. My mouth is locked, and I am throwing away the key, you see." Says Kalei. They return to their cabin, deciding they have had enough water for the day.

Chapter Eleven

HydroKnox and the Dangers Lurking in the Dark

It's the last evening of camp, the girls sense a final adventure is in order. Late in the evening, the staff and fellow campers in their cabin go to sleep, The girls sneak out to the Cove to reflect on the strange occurrences of the weekend.

They kick off their shoes and walk to the end of the pier, sit at the edge, and dangle their feet over the dock into the water, as they have done many times before. However, this time, they no longer feel a sense of peace emanating from the Cove. Instead, an unsettling feeling of malaise envelops them, hovering like a mist settling over a meadow in the dead of night.

As the girls sit in silence, the sound of crashing waves begins to echo around them. The noise grows louder, more powerful, until it becomes almost deafening, filling the air with tension. Unease creeps over them.

"Kalei… do you hear that?" Willow's voice wavers as she tugs on Kalei's shirt.

Kalei glances toward the water. "Yeah… I hear it. Do you see those ripples?"

"I do," Willow nods, her eyes scanning the surface. "But I can't tell where they're coming from. Can you?"

Kalei narrows her gaze, straining to see. "No… I can't either."

The ripples in the water are now reaching them, it is becoming more evident that something out in the cove is causing a commotion. The girls strain their eyes ever more, trying to determine what is causing it.

Suddenly, a large shape emerges from the water and returns to the water with a small splash, causing the girls to fall on their backs on the pier in fear. They get a glimpse of a massive sea creature, its blue-greenish scales glinting in the moonlight. This creature measures about 8 feet long and 3 feet wide.

The ripples disrupt the calm water at the pier where the girls sit. They gaze out to the break point of the Cove.

They observe two luminous balls of light descending from the top of the water, their colors shifting as they shimmer in the night.

The duo are astonished by the unfolding spectacle.

Suddenly, the two balls of light vanish, replaced by a quick splash about 5 feet away that engulfs their legs up to their knees, paralyzing them with shock.

"Kalei!... What is that?"

DC Daniel

"I don't know…. Ahhhhh!" screams Kalei.

Out of nowhere, a creature emerges from the Cove, its two glowing balls on his head. Surprisingly, the beast is not a dreadful or hideous sea monster as it moves closer, but rather the opposite - it exhibits a calming aura that instantly puts the girls at ease.

HydroKnox emerges with a gentle smile; the creature captivates the girls with its sleek and smooth indigo exterior, adorned with hints of teal and blue that sparkle in the light. The interwoven scales create a blend into a sleek scaling armor. This armor interweaves into the creature's water-repellent skin like a seal.

This creature looks unique in the moonlight with its yellow eyes, cat-like mouth, and nose. It also has cool green ears that pulsate in a sea-green glow; each ear turns 90 degrees back and forth. These large ears are like an echolocation system, telling depth and distance.

The girls are curious and dumbfounded. They look at each other to guess where this creature comes from.

While they both think back to class last week about Nessie, the Loch Ness monster, they have never encountered a creature like this before.

This creature speaks as it locks eyes with Kalei.

"Hello, my name is HydroKnox. I am from the depths of the sea, and I am your water guardian, protector, and one of the special keepers of the sea."

The girls are in awe of this wondrous creature and the secrets it holds from the depths below.

"What do you want from us, HydroKnox?"

"I want to take you and Willow on a magical adventure out past the cove in the sea."

"Kalei, I don't know about this. I am adventurous but letting this sea creature take us out to sea for a party—This is a joke right? Its nor safe? We can't swim underwater!"

"Willow, you can trust me; I am Kalei's water guardian and protect anyone around her, too. Trust me…" he says with a smile and a twinkle in his eye.

Kalei jumps in the water, "Come on in, Willow. Don't be a chicken little!"

"Kalei, why must you be so rude and try to guilt-trip me into following you? I am perfectly fine right here, on the pier. WHERE I CAN BREATHE.

I am not going in unless you wanna share some super underwater power to breathe. Last I checked, we weren't heirs to the DNA of Aquaman."

"It's peer pressure. You'll be fine. Now come on, Willow, put your big girl pants on and JUMP IN!."

Eventually, Willow jumps in, and both girls climb onto HydroKnox's back, feeling the scaly but silky-smooth skin and cool touch of the creature's body.

HydroKnox has fin-like foot holsters emerging from his sides.

They step in, and it wraps around their feet, providing stability and security.

"Kalei….Willow, are you ready?" asks HydroKnox.

The girls grab onto the dorsal fins before them and prepare to embark on their adventure. With a burst of energy, HydroKnox begins its ascent out past the Cove into the ocean's open waters, gaining speed and weaving in and out of the water like a serpent, leaving the Cove behind.

The moonlight shimmers on the water, grabbing the girls' attention. But they can't help noticing the glowing antennas sticking out from the yellow, glowing circles on its head.

As the antennas bounce around and touch each other, they make a sizzling sound, like electricity.

Willow gazes down at the water below, noticing her reflection rippling in the moonlight. She tips her hand out, gliding atop the water.

Willow shouts with exhilaration as she floats across the water. "Whoa! WAHOOO! I FEEL LIKE I CAN FLY!"

Willow is experiencing a newfound sense of freedom. She doesn't feel tethered or restricted for the first time in her life.

Doubt fills her mind, making her wonder if this is even real. She thinks, "Is this just another one of my dreams?

Did I imagine this magical creature?" Willow reaches out and pinches Kalei. "Do you feel that?"

"Ouch! YES, I feel it! You're so weird… That really hurt!"

Kalei pinches Willow's back. "Do YOU feel that?!"

"Ouch! YES, I feel it. I guess I'm not dreaming anymore."

Reality hits them—they're riding a friendly sea serpent out of the Cove and into the wide-open ocean. It feels just like a scene from one of her fantasy books. Relaxing, the girls fully embrace the adventure, letting the serpent guide them to this ocean party.

As they move farther from the Cove, they start to feel small compared to the huge ocean around them.

They watch in amazement as the serpent slices through the water effortlessly, like a hot knife through butter, creating a smooth and unreal experience.

After traveling for a while, they turn around and realize the Cove's lights have disappeared.

All they see are little white waves on the moonlit ocean, stretching out as far as they can see.

Suddenly, Willow's curiosity takes over, and she shouts to the sea serpent, "Where are you taking us?"

"I'm taking you and Kalei to see everything at the bottom of the ocean," it replies.

"Are you going to drown us? Are we going to be fish food?" Willow asks nervously.

"No, silly! There's an underwater playground where my family and friends live. I want to share this magical place with both of you."

The group approaches a small beam of light in the distance. HydroKnox asks. "Can you both swim?"

Kalei looks at Willow and asks. "Willow, you can swim…. right?"

"uhm like this is a great time ask, out in the middle of the ocean. Of Course, I can swim.

Don't you remember us going past the breaking point when your mom took us swimming at Anna Maria Island?"

"Yes, yes, I remember. I love Coquina Beach."

HydroKnox gives a short, loud whistle.

"Phweeett."

"Phweeett."

"OK, both of you must jump off and swim under the water. Keep holding your breath."

"Kalei, I told you this was a bad idea. We won't survive; we are not fish; we can't breathe underwater."

"Don't worry, rest assured, the two of you. When you jump off and swim underwater, I will blow a special oxygen bubble over your head.

This bubble will remain with us in the water, providing you two with oxygen to breathe."

Upon hearing this, Willow becomes uneasy, and her pessimistic thoughts take over. She doubts the plan, but HydroKnox reassures them that he controls everything.

"Kalei, Willow, this is how it will work. The oxygen bubble I am providing has a sticky ceiling substance that would seal to the bottom of your neck.

This will prevent it from popping into the water. This thick film produces an unlimited source of oxygen; it will last until you two resurface above the ocean."

"OK, Kalei, that makes as much sense as a screen door in a submarine. Physics and water pressure.

Hydro, how do I know you're telling the truth? And this is not some evil plan to grab us and take us down deep in the water, drown us, and feed out lifeless bodies to your youngest in your feeding lair?"

"Willow, quit fussing. It's OK; stop worrying. Remember YOLO…. You only live once. Remember BFF for life? I feel it in my gut. Everything will be fine," says Kalei.

Willow gives Kalei a frightened look on their face. "OK….
OK…. Kalei, I trust you, but I am not sure I trust your
friend."

Willow grabs Kalei's pinky finger and speaks. "BFF
FOREVER… Let's do this!"

Chapter Twelve

Bubbles, Serpents, and Secrets

As the girls count down together, they synchronize their movements and dive into the waves. HydroKnox responds by producing the first oxygen bubble from its antennas.

Kalei quickly swims towards the bubble. While Willow patiently holds her breath, HydroKnox clicks his antennas again, producing one more bubble.

Willow quickly swims toward it. The girls easily enter the bubbles and look at each other, feeling a sense of relief and excitement.

The girls meet eye-to-eye and exchange a watery high five, feeling grateful for each other's company and excited for the adventure ahead.

Willow then points downward, and Kalei catches sight of the ocean floor. The surprise on her face is evident, but instinct takes over. She takes a big breath, ready to swim down, and realizes she can breathe normally. Looking down, they see the stunning marine life beneath them.

Willow then gives Kalei a thumbs up and points towards the bottom, to which Kalei nods and starts swimming in that direction. HydroKnox leads the way, with the two girls holding on to his fins. As they swim, a large school of Royal Blue Tang glides past them.

Soon, they reach a point where two serpents that resemble HydroKnox but are smaller in size greet the girls.

HydroKnox introduces them as his twin children and instructs the girls to grab onto one of their fins as they take them deeper into the ocean, where a party is happening.

The girls follow the directive, grabbing the fins, while HydroKnox's children follow his lead and dive deeper and deeper into the ocean.

In that fleeting moment, the party has begun; the ocean is alive with joy and merrymaking.

The two young serpent creatures swim away, and the girls join the festivities, looking at the interactions.

The girls look right; they see three octopuses playing volleyball with a happy pufferfish and a makeshift seaweed net. Blue crabs are square dancing with each other at the edge of the sandbar.

The girls swim a little downstream; they see the yellow tangs play keep-away with a rock, projecting it from their mouths while another tang catches it in the distance, making sure the fish friend in the middle does not intercept it. Willow watches baby stingrays playing hide-and-seek.

The hiders flutter their bodies into the sand until fully submerged, while the seeker stingray glides over the sea floor and flutters its body to uncover the hiding playmates.

Kalei views a pack of seahorses circling a large oyster that is upright in a vertical position. The clam suddenly ejects a pearl, and the seahorses play a game of soccer pearl.

The red or blue teams pass it from one team member to another, avoiding the opposing team.

With skill and muscle, they use their torso to pass it to another seahorse, making their way down the ocean field to the goal line for points.

The goalie is two crabs, one on each side of the arena. Two electrifying eels keep score on the seaweed scoreboard.

The sidelines fill with other electrical eels, seahorses, dolphins, and starfish.

The girls swim around, taking in all the wonders that surround them. HydroKnox is always nearby; within a few flips of a dolphin's tail, they enjoy the adventure their new serpent friend bestows.

What feels like minutes turns into hours. In the distance, the girls hear the cries of whales and the clicking sound of a pod of dolphins.

As the time for departure arrives, HydroKnox approaches the girls and informs Kalei that though their adventure has been plentiful, it's time to return to the Cove.

Kalei signals to Willow by tapping her shoulder and mouthing the words.

"It's time to go."

They both take hold of HydroKnox's dorsal fins, with a dart they ascend swiftly toward the ocean's surface as their heads emerge from the water.

Pop!

Pop!

Once again, the girls mount HydroKnox and hold on tightly as they begin their journey back to the Cove.

"Kalei, I can see the shore, look!"

"Yes, we are getting closer."

Suddenly, out of nowhere, a screeching sound, like nails on a chalkboard. As the sound pierces the air, it is followed by a rush of air that nearly knocks Willow off HydroKnox.

They look up and see a gigantic Pfizer bird coming straight toward them, screeching and reaching its talons out to grab one of them.

In a moment of quick thinking, Kalei and Willow jump off HydroKnox and stay afloat in the water. Willow can see the beady little red eyes headed straight toward her.

A prehistoric gargantuan Pfizer Pelican continues to swoop down toward them, with Willow as its target. Willow dives underwater. The Pfizer misses her as its talons go into the water, trying desperately to grab her.

HydroKnox then appears halfway out of the water, emitting a loud clicking sound as it propels itself toward the Pfizer.

Willow and Kalei watch in awe as HydroKnox sprays the bird with a red liquid unfamiliar to them. Then, it covers the bird's wingspan, causing it to freeze and crumble into tiny ice chunks instantly.

The ice chunks hit the water with a sizzling sound, about 20 feet away from the girls.

The girls are frightened by the sudden attack, having only expected to participate in a fun adventure and party on the ocean floor. They never expected to be attacked by a giant prehistoric Pfizer with such a huge wingspan.

"Thank you HydroKnox. We are grateful for your quick thinking and action in saving Willow from harm.

HydroKnox approaches the girls.

"Remember, Kalei. I am your protector and guardian, protecting you and your friend. Now quickly jump on my back. We need to get you two back to safety, pronto."

Chapter Thirteen

Last Day at Camp

The girls comply and settle in for the rest of the journey. He effortlessly carries them through the water, safely bringing them back to the dock where they had started.

With the strength of his serpent body, he arches his back and lifts them onto the platform. The girls dismount, grateful for the adventure and protection that their water friend provides.

"Thank you, HydroKnox, for your protection, but why did the bird attack me?"

Hydro says. "You know, Willow, you're a special girl; you have powers so great that many want you dead."

"What? Why? I am a nobody; I was left in the hospital. Jeesh! My own mom didn't want me, I was unloved and abandoned.

And what the heck is up with the bird's beady little red eyes?

"Well, little lady, sometimes things get possessed by evil powers, and I believe when someone's or something's eyes turn solid black or red, they are possessed creatures. Someone sent it on a mission to destroy you."

Kalei says. "I don't understand why they would want to hurt her."

"Not to worry, you two; soon enough, it will all make sense; just stay safe and have patience."

 "Come on, Willow, we must return to the cabin."

"Yes, let's hurry. I am so freaking out. This evening has been a blessing and a curse."

Before HydroKnox departs, he says, "We will meet again in your future water-related adventures. He then spits out a beautiful shell with interweaved streaks of purple and teal and says, "Kalei, blow it whenever you need me, or you are in grave danger."

"What is this HydroKnox, I don't understand.?"

"Kalei, just give it a blow and it will make a sound,"

She gives it a blow, listening as it produces an echoing up-and-down melody.

"That's it, just like that, I am with you always."

The girls say their goodbyes as they kiss HydroKnox's head. He leaps backward with a joyful splash, sinking back into the water and spinning sideways like a spinner dolphin before swimming out of the Cove.

The girls watch him go, giggling with happiness. "Come on, let's get back,"

Willow says. "Yeah, I don't want to be out here anymore; the fun is over."

The girls return to the cabin, still feeling the remnants of their ocean adventure clinging to their skin.

They quietly enter the cabin, careful not to wake their sleeping cabinmates.

The scent of sea salt and seaweed adheres to them, a reminder of the unforgettable experience they just went through. They quickly gather their towels and toiletries and go to the showers to wash off the night's adventures.

As they wash up, Willow says. "I am trying to process why the crazy Pfizer Pelican was targeting me. It was huge, like I have never seen a bird that big."

"IDK, my Tutu never told me about evil birds or possessed people. Whatever it is, I think we should talk to my mom when we get back home."

"Yes, she may know something; your **tūtū** is her Grandparent, right?"

"Yes, maybe my **tūtū wahine** told her of this, or maybe she has seen something like it before."

"Now you just added another word… **wahine,** What's that?"

"my **tūtū wahine** means Grandmother. I usually just call her **tūtū** for short."

The girls finish their shower, they pause for a moment, listening carefully. A soft sound seems to fill the air, like a distant song.

DC Daniel

Chapter Fourteen

HydroKnox's Secret

"Willow, do you hear the whales calling?" Kalei asks.

It was a strange, beautiful noise—low and echoing, like the voice of something deep and powerful far out in the ocean. The sound felt like a mystery, as if the whales were speaking in their own secret language, trying to communicate from beneath the waves.

"Yeah, Kalei, do you hear the dolphins clicking? Amazingly, we can hear this, not being in the water, or next to the clove."

"Yeah, what's going on out there? It's like we are connected somehow with HydroKnox." Kalei says, looking off in the distance to the Cove.

Exhausted from the night's adventure, the girls make their way back to the cabin, catching glimpses of the sunrise on the horizon.

When they arrive, the other girls are just waking up and are curious about why Willow and Kalei are up so early. The girls explain that they want to shower before heading out to morning meditation. Despite their tiredness, the girls know they have an unforgettable experience that will stay with them for a long time. All the girls from cabin nine gather their yoga mats and head down to the Cove for morning meditation.

They meet up with Trinity and settle into a circle facing the beautiful Cove. Miss Simmons, this radiant Indian Zen lady, always leads the group.

Kalei hears splashing in the Cove and hears HydroKnox's subliminal message, "I'm always here."

DC Daniel

She taps Willow's leg and silently points to the Cove. Willow's eyes widen as she looks towards the horizon and sees HydroKnox.

He briefly pops his head out of the water. However, they both notice that no one else seems to be aware of his presence.

Two friends look at each other, share a secret look, and grab each other's pinky, silently sealing their best friend Pac.

Then, they close their eyes and return to peaceful thinking. They both feel calm and safe because they believe HydroKnox is looking out for them as they meditate.

The sun fully makes its appearance, making everything around them look glowing and warm.

After the morning meditation, the camp leaders instruct all the kids to head to the field and locate their designated cones. There, they will discover various games, followed by a chance to create their sundae at the lunch tent.

The campers spend the rest of the morning playing tug of war, water balloon toss, and other fun relay races.

The kids laugh and shout, thoroughly enjoying the activities and the beautiful weather. After the races, the counselors set up an ice cream sundae social in the lunch tent. The campers are overjoyed as they pile on their favorite toppings and enjoy their sweet treats.

As the Day goes on, the kids pack up their belongings and prepare to leave camp. The counselors gather everyone together for a final goodbye ceremony.

Miss Simmons gives a heartfelt speech, "I know that everyone has had an awesome time; I will miss all of you. Until we meet again, everyone, let's pile together for a big ole' snowball group hug.

As the bus pulls away from camp, the girls of cabin nine wave goodbye to their new friend and the beautiful Cove. They feel deep satisfaction and fulfillment, knowing they experienced something special with HydroKnox.

Chapter Fifteen
(Order of the 12 Elements)

Willow awakens to the aroma of hot cakes and coffee filling the house. She springs out of bed and rushes downstairs to investigate, greeted by her mother's smile, a morning greeting, and an embrace.

"Good morning, Sunshine. Did you sleep well? I must say, I am so glad you had a terrific time; I am sure it was a great getaway. Did anything exciting happen at camp?"

"Yes, I slept very well; I missed my bed so much. Sleeping on camp bunk mats was like sleeping in a tree."

"Wow, I am sorry to hear that… however, you must have had an amazing time. What exciting stuff did you all do?"

"Mom, it was the best weekend ever. Kalei and I participated in archery, horseback riding, and relay games, and we got to go swimming."

"Later that night, they settled in at the dinner table to enjoy the delicious meal that her mother had prepared: a delicious fare of Salisbury steak, baked potato, and a cucumber, tomato, feta salad with a drizzle of Greek dressing. Her mother asks as they endearingly converse about the past weekend's events.

"Is there anything else you wish to share? Did you meet anyone new?"

Willow has a choked look on her face. Thinking back to the kids at the group home and being told she was a liar or cheat.

Especially when she would tell off-the-wall stories, or when something came up missing in the house, her mind is racing in thought,

"I don't think she'll understand if I talk about the magical stuff. She might not believe me and call me a liar. What if she sends me away because she didn't see it herself?" So Willow keeps silent about her experiences and answers. "Umm… Uhhh…… No! Not really, just the stuff kids do at camp."

Willow's mom can see the distress on her daughter's face. Willow is usually truthful; she doesn't want to feel rejected or cast away by her mother, so she tries to change the subject by saying.

"At camp, I met a new girl named Trinity; I didn't even know she existed in our school or group."

Willow feels like she needs to expel her magical experiences to someone. She thinks, *"I should be able to tell her anything. So, what do I have to fear? I guess my foster care experiences are holding me back.* Emotions play back in her mind. *That darn girl Tina, always telling me, shut up, Weepy Willow, no one wants to hear your dumb thoughts."*

She looks at her mother, wanting to give it a try. She asks.

"Mom, you are not going to send me away, if what I tell you something, so off the wall. Something that can't be explained, and you probably won't understand?"

"No dear, of course not. You're here for good. No matter what kiddo. I love you, and I always will."

"Ok Mom here goes nothing, have you ever heard of the twelve elements?"

"Yes, like some of the elements on the periodic table? I think there were more than twelve, dear."

"No Mom, like the Elements that our universe ticks to… like ***Earth, Wind, Fire, Water, and the Moon***? You see I think we are all connected at a cosmic level."

"I have heard of the four elements of nature, such as earth, water, wind, and fire, but I am unsure of the other elements you mentioned. Why do you ask, dear?"

"Well, Mom, I had this crescent moon appear on my hand at camp; it's followed by this strange surge of energy and warm feeling, almost burning in my hand. The top of my hand was illuminating and glowing this moon symbol."

Her mother gasps but tries to stay calm and not show her feelings. She waits until her daughter finishes talking and then asks her a question "Have you ever experienced this before?"

"Yes, ma'am, a few weeks before camp came, Kalei and I sat on the balcony, and my hand was glowing.

When it happens, I can feel the energy pulsing through my body. I never saw the Crescent moon appear until camp; I thought it was just a fluke. Kalei was there; she saw it, too. What do you think is going on, mum?"

"I'm not sure, Willow, but whatever it is, I know you'll come out stronger because of it."

Willow's mother asks another prying question. "What happen with this moon shape you were talking about?"

"Mom, you promise you won't send me away if I tell you something else?"

"My dear child, what nonsense are you speaking of? I would never send you away; I love you and I am here for you; you can tell me anything."

"OK, you have to pinky swear."

They both hold their pinkies, "I pinky swear, Willow."

"OK, well, it's like this; at camp, when Kalei and I were at morning meditation, we found ourselves hovering above our mats, and … as strange as it sounds, Kalei had a luminous mark appear on her hand too… Then we met a strange gray-haired lady that disappeared into thin air, not before she told Kalei and I, that we are special."

She waits for a few moments for a response from her mom. Her mother can't help her face; it tells it all: shock and disbelief. Her jaw gapes open as if she just saw a ghost; she is left speechless for a few seconds, and what her mom can get out in sounds. It is like she is stuttering to find her words.

"Ma… may …. maybe…… it's some kind of ma... magic; I am sure everything will be fine. There is no... not... noth nothing to worry about, you should talk to Kalei's mom about this. Willow, you know, Mrs. Applegate asked me if we would join her for dinner tomorrow. Do you want to attend?"

"That would be delightful, I hope she has some answers."

Chapter Sixteen

A Taste of Magic

Willow meets up with her friends Kalei and Trinity at school the following day, and they embrace each other tightly as if they have been separated for a long time, even though it's only been less than 48 hours since they returned from camp.

While walking towards their science class, Willow leans towards Kalei's ear and whispers, "Did anything unusual occur last night." Kalei shakes her head, indicating that nothing out of the ordinary happened. The girls proceed to their classes and finish the day.

Kalei has permission to stay after school with Willow, and they meet up in her mom's classroom. Miss Juno packs up, and the trio makes their way to Kalei's house.

Upon arriving at her friend's house, the girls rush in, leaving Willow's mother behind.

Willow's mother greets her friend, Mrs. Applegate, with a warm embrace and a hug, while Miss Juno hands over bottled water and a bunt cake as a dinner gift. Mrs. Applegate expresses her gratitude and welcomes her into her home. Meanwhile, the moms engage in small talk at the kitchen table.

The girls enter the kitchen, cheery and talkative as usual, and offer their assistance.

"Yes, girls, please set the table, **keiki**; your father is coming home soon."

Moments later, Sarah announces. "Everything is ready for dinner. I am waiting for your **makua kāne,... keiki**."

Just then, Mr. Applegate arrives home from work; Stephen is a stalky fellow with a handlebar mustache and beard nearly covering his bottom lip.

He greets his wife and heads to his office with his briefcase. Mrs. Applegate announces from the kitchen,

"We will have Hawaiian chicken with pigeon peas in rice, and Miss Juno brought over a deliciously smelling bundt cake."

"Thank you, ladies, it sounds delicious. I need a few more minutes to respond to an important email.

One of my workers need important information, before joining dinner. I won't be more than 5 minutes."

While they wait, everyone sits at the table playing the roundtable game, inquiring how each of their days went. The girls respond with their upcoming tests and current grades.

Clara talks about how her day goes with grading papers and instructing the kids at school. Stephen joins the conversation, and speaks of his next forthcoming contract, which will take place this summer in Hawaii, to upgrade the island's telecommunications.

Kalei takes over the table with overflowing excitement about the upcoming trip and how she will see her **Ohana** back on the island, by the North Shore.

The five of them enjoyed the delicious dinner, and the girls finished their meals quickly, eager to leave the table and continue their conversations in Kalei's room.

They discuss various topics, playing Fortnite and scrolling through their social media profiles.

Mr. Applegate completes his meal. "Honey, I need to return to my office;

I just got another text about some blueprints for the new data center rollout." Smiling with a smirk, he then jokes with them.

"This will give you two hens in the henhouse plenty of time to chat and gossip." He quietly leaves the room, leaving the women to continue to conversate.

Mrs. Applegate once again mentions the girls coming of age to Miss Juno and further explains the magical things that happen at camp to the girls. Miss Juno is taken aback by this even though she knows what Willow told her.

"Clara, have you noticed anything strange about Willows' behavior? Has she made mention, of anything out of the ordinary?"

Miss Juno is unsure how to react to the statement because she is unaware that Mrs. Applegate has any deep knowledge of this topic of magic, other than the brief conversation with the girls getting to camp. Sarah's speech inquires as if she is nudging Clara for something. She remains composed and unaffected by Mrs. Applegate's questioning about Willow. Her face remains like a clean slate with no facial expression from these probing questions.

Miss Applegate asks again. "Clara, have you noticed anything strange or unusual about Willow?"

"I can't think of anything, Sarah. Why do you keep asking me this?"

"Because Kalei told me some things happened on their adventures at camp. I feel that Willow enlightened you on something, so spill the milk."

"I do believe the girls are special and different, but I don't believe they have magical powers."

Miss Applegate spends the next 5 minutes explaining that her family has a history of magic. That they are part of a group of **extra~ordinary** celestial beings.

"You see, these powers typically manifest around the magical 13th birthday. You know Kalei's birthday is on July 13th, and she will be turning 13, which is the age when magical powers usually start to develop."

Miss Juno looks at Mrs. Applegate with confusion and disbelief, unsure what to make of this revelation about magical powers.

Sarah elaborates further. "My family has a long and rich history of practicing Wixans, becoming powerful ones at the magic school.

"What a Magic School, are you serious right now? This isn't real, I didn't just adopt a magical girl. Bah humbug. Get right with me Sarah."

No, Clara, I am straight up with you, so here is more of the story. These special people like our family and others.

They keep this world safe from what you and I know as evil and cursed spirits, that want to harm others. We typically only use our powers to help or protect others. This is a long generation of family from my husband and my family. We all follow the same rules and practice being kind."

"Ok, I don't believe what I am hearing, but go on."

 Sarah gently grabs Clara's hand and says, "We have 7 simple rules.

#1. Use your powers to help others, and never against free will.

#2. Honor the secret book of MANA and the Emerald Tablets.

#3. Act as if you are a child of the Universe.

#4. Treat your own body as if it were a temple.

#5. Be kind and thoughtful and live with gratitude.

#6. Believe in yourself.

#7 Always be kind, patient, and honest with all humans."

"Ok, but these rules are simple, but what's a Wixan, and how is that magical?"

"It's hard to explain to a Glyphless one, but what I can tell you is there are people in this world with special powers given by the Order of the 12 Elements. And the girls are like the rest of the Wixan's."

So like you're a witch and your husbands a wizard?"

Well, I don't identify as a witch or wizard… I rather say, I am a Wixan.

"Clara have you ever caused harm or hurt someone?"

"Juno, you know, I have never had to use my powers to fight the dark forces; I have heard stories of great wizards and enchantresses embarking on a journey with amulets, potions, and the book of the divine.

They brought their foretellers, transmuters, and abjurers to help rid out the dark forces of Evil.

The exceptional powers of Sorcerer Panick guided them; they kept The Nordic School of Craft safe and open for all the kids to continue to attend."

"Juno, you know, I received my powers just after I turned 13, I have been honing in on them ever since."

Clara listens more intently, still unsure of what to believe.

"Here Clara, maybe this will help you understand. What the Fire Element is." She begins to initiate a spell. Sarah, looking as if it is a mundane task, unenthused, waves her hand and speaks.

"firemortus"

A small flame appears in the palm of her hand. Miss Juno gasps in amazement, unable to explain what she sees.

She begins to realize that there is more to the world than she has ever imagined and that there is some truth to Mrs. Applegate's claims of divine powers.

Chapter Seventeen

Trinity Bends Space & Time

The girls are having such a blast on May 23rd, their last day of school!

The day fills up with relay races, balloon tosses, the dart-throwing game, hitting the target, and the ultimate highlight—dumping the principal in the water tank.

Mrs. Sandalwood, one of Kalei's favorite teachers, is in charge of the popcorn machine. Mr. Kouts, Willow's beloved gym teacher, serves delicious rainbow snow cones. The girls are having the time of their lives!

Mr. Sanchez comes on the PA. "Billy Baxter and Federico Barcelona, please report to the stage. The blueberry Pie Eating contest starts in 20 minutes."

In the days leading up to the contest, a cohort of children threw their names into the ring.

Among them, two figures emerged: Billy Baxter, the school bully, whose companions consisted solely of his two henchmen and a handful of loyal minion followers.

And the other winner, Federico Barcelona, celebrated by the whiz kid collective, this boy is universally adored.

Hailing from Spain, Federico's intellect surpasses that of his peers, and his benevolence endears him to all.

Unlike Billy, who garnered disdain, Federico is described by his peers as having affability, an outgoing nature, and unwavering support for the marginalized underdogs.

With a sneer, Billy remarks, "You're so slim and slender; there's no way you could win this contest. You're too bony and stringy—I bet you can't even get through one pie if you try."

With a confident smirk, Federico retorts, "Well, Thomas, at least my chances of winning aren't as slim as your taste in insults. Let's see if your words are as hollow as your pie-eating skills. Bring it on!"

The two boys sit down at their contestant spots. Mr. Sanchez gets on his megaphone and announces the starting point.

Everybody is in front and beside the tables, watching this epic showdown.

"Are you two ready?... Okay, remove your masks, get set, and on the count of one begin! Five, four, three, two, begin!"

Standing there in amazement, the school bully digs in with both hands; Federico keeps pace.

Trinity giggles, envisioning a humorous scenario, she says to her friends, "Imagine if bully Baxter picks up that pie and dumps it on his head."

Kalei, in a condescending tone, adds, "Trinity, it would be even funnier if he acts like a pig and makes a complete fool of himself."

Trinity lightly giggles, amused by Kalei's remarks, and goes into a dead-stare trance with Billy, whispering to herself, "So, how do you like this… Bully Baxter?"

As they watch the scene unfold, Trinity continues her dead stare, now making a figure 8 with her index finger in the air.

She leans in, closer to the table, her voice dropping to a lower soft, almost magical murmur. "Fool and fumble, trip and tumble—pie on your face, let chaos rumble."

Willow bursts into laughter as Baxter's ears start to grow, and then his mouth transforms into a snout. The crowd roars hysterically as they witness him snorting pig sounds.

Trinity giggles to herself; Willow snaps her fingers at her face. "Trinity, snap out of it! Do you see what's happening?"

At that moment, Trinity returns to reality; she sees her daydream come to life.

Thomas dumps an entire blueberry pie on his head while playing the tap drums on the tin pan still attached to his head, with blueberry filling dripping everywhere.

Grabbing a second pie, Thomas acts just as Trinity imagined.

He looks at the crowd, makes pig snorting sounds, and smears his face into the pie like a pig. The crowd laughs even louder, and the judges come running.

"Thomas, are you OK?" they ask.

Thomas looks up, channels his inner pig, and proudly declares, "I've officially gone hog wild! My wig's on vacation, and I'm the blueberry pie maestro. Bawhhaaa Haaa Haa… Snort snort... Oink-credible, right?

Thomas looks up, snorts like a pig, and exclaims, "I've turned into a porktastic spectacle! I lost my bully marbles … Snort snort... Oink! Oink! Oh yeah, I'm living my best piggy life!"

By now, the entire crowd is rolling with laughter. Mr. Sanchez pays no more attention to Thomas and walks over to Federico.

"Boy, stand up! You are the winner due to Billy going pig crazy," he announces, raising his left hand. "Federico Barcelona, you are the 2020 pie-eating contest winner."

Trinity has not fully grasped what she has just done.

In that moment, Kalei chimed in, saying, "That's the funniest thing I've seen in ages. Looks like our school bully won't be causing any more trouble. I mean, who'd take him seriously after he's turned himself into a walking joke in front of the entire school? Graduating with 'fun`niwsh… dungus pig' on his diploma? Classic!"

The girls burst into laughter, but it left Trinity deep in thought. *"Can this really happen? I have never seen my thoughts become reality."*

Chapter Eighteen

Superpowers, Sleepovers, and Surprises

Later that night the group meets up at Trinity's house for a slumber party.

Trinity is a taller-than-normal teen her age with shoulder-length black hair that she often wears in pigtails or in space buns. Trinity is the reserved quiet type but good friends with Willow and Kalei.

The trio grabs their bikes and backpacks to head to the Princess Preserve Forest Park. The movie on stage tonight is "A Wrinkle in Time". Three peculiar beings go to its third dimension of space to find Meg's father. Bending space and time to get the girl's father back. They spread out the Peach blanket and all settled in to watch the movie.

After the movie, they gather their stuff and head back to Trinity's for the slumber party.

As the girls settle in for their slumber party, Trinity can't shake the feeling that what happened at the blueberry pie eating contest was more than just a coincidence. She decides to share her thoughts with Willow and Kalei.

"I know this might sound crazy, but I think I have some sort of magic power," Trinity said tentatively."

"What do you mean?" Kalei asked, intrigued.

"I mean, I had this funny thought about Thomas dumping a pie on his head and acting like a pig, and then it happened right in front of my eyes, it was like I was in a trance," Trinity explains. Willow and Kalei exchange a skeptical glance, as Trinity continues.

"And then, when we were watching the trailer for 'A Wrinkle in Time,' I had this strange feeling like I could bend space and time, by making people do silly antics."

"Trinity conspires, "Like, what if I could use my thoughts to make things happen?"

The girls were quiet for a moment, considering Trinity's words. Then, Kalei spoke up.

 "Well, if you really do have magic powers, then maybe we can help you figure out how to use them!" Kalei exclaims.

 "Yeah, we could be like a team of superheroes, using our special powers to make the world a better place," Willow adds.

The girls play thoughts off, one another, brainstorming ideas for how the powers could help other people. They talk about stopping school bullies, healing sick animals, and even traveling back in time to fix past mistakes.

Trinity could not help but think about what had happened at school earlier.

She had always known she had telepathic abilities, but she never thought they could have such a tangible effect on the world around her.

As the group is getting ready for bed, Kalie and Willow could almost see the wheels turning in Trinity's mind, just like when she slipped into one of her trances.

It was the same look she'd had during the school pie contest with Bully Baxter.

Willow and Kalei stared in wide-eyed disbelief as Trinity's thoughts start to take shape around them.

"Uh, Trinity… what's with this purple mist swirling around us?" Willow asks, her voice trembling a little.

Kalei glances at Willow, feeling uneasy. "Yeah, something feels really weird. Wait—Willow, you're floating!"

Willow gasps. "Bogie Barnacles! We all are!"

"Holy Moley… this is amazing!" Trinity exclaims, a huge grin spreading across her face.

"They are all defying gravity with ease, laughter bubbling up from them as they spin weightlessly. Trinity couldn't believe how incredible it felt."

As the night goes on, the trio continues to act strangely, they all have a fun time. The girls dance around the room, making up their own silly language like using Pig Latin and telling jokes that make no sense.

Trinity realizes that her telepathic abilities could be a source of endless entertainment. She vows to use them for good and to always bring a smile to the faces of those around her.

They drift off to sleep, as Trinity's eyes wander the room. She feels a sense of excitement and possibility.

She doesn't know if there's any merit to her abilities, or if she has magic powers or not, but the idea of being part of something larger that could change the world was thrilling.

And who knows, maybe they would even find a way to bend space and time, just like in the movie. Anything seems possible at this moment, and Trinity knows that she is ready for whatever adventures lay ahead.

They all drift off to sleep, exhausted but happy. Trinity falls into a dreamland excited to see what other adventures her telepathic abilities will lead her on in the future.

Teaser Chapter

Chapter One

Three Girls,

One Extraordinary Destiny

Sarah, I understand you say you have these special powers; what do you think the girls' powers will be?

"It's difficult to predict for either of the girls. So far, they've only revealed a single hieroglyphic sign.

If they don't uncover it before they arrive, they will receive their elemental assignment and learn how to harness their true Universal powers."

"Powers, you mean they get multiple powers?"

"Juno, you know, there are 12 elements if they haven't figured it out.

It will be okay because when they arrive at the Manu'ahi Summit, we will stop by Professor SpellBee's Spellbinding Sticks, and she will assist them. Until then, it's anybody's guess."

Miss Juno seems to comprehend and understand what Mrs. Applegate is telling her.

"Juno, you know, in the world of magic, we call someone like you a glyphless one."

"Why do you keep saying 'Juno, you know?'"

"Well, it rhymes! And since you're a teacher with so much knowledge, it feels fitting to say it that way—with kindness and affection."

"Ha! I suppose that makes sense…"

While Mrs. Applegate is explaining things, the two girls are upstairs, thinking about all the strange stuff happening to them. They remember the glowing symbols that appeared on their skin, meeting HydroKnox, and how Kalei used her waterpowers to save a kid from drowning. They also think about how they floated above their yoga mats during meditation and the mysterious woman, Gabriella, in the forest.

Then there's Trinity, with her crazy powers—she can make things float with zero gravity and even change people's thoughts. Everything is so confusing and puzzling for them.

"You know Willow, my **kupuna,** or as you all say here in Florida, Grandpa. He would tell me a story called the awakening of the soul.

When a young girl or boy hits a certain age, they may have the ability to tap into their elemental magic.

He would tell me, one day, my **keiki**, you will find your path; I see it in you; your ability to shine and give positive high vibrations.

This is one of the many unique characteristics that make you extraordinary, my dear **keiki**."

Willow and Kalei continue to chat, excited about the supernatural events of the last few weeks.

Willow says to Kalei, "You are my best friend in the whole wide world. No matter what we go through, the up's and the downs, I want us to remain soul sisters."

"Ditto Willow, you are the sister I never had, you know, I heard this once from a famous person. You've heard of Franklin Roosevelt, right? He was one of the presidents.

Anyway, in his big speech in 1933, he said something like, 'We have nothing to fear but fear itself.' So, I'm ready to check out these elemental powers. What about you?"

"So, you're saying we have to face our fears and take action, even if we're unsure about the future?" Kalei asks.

Willow smiles and nods. She reaches out her pinky, and Kalei locks hers in a pinky swear.

"Alright, I'm in! Let's make this future full of awesome adventures!"

The girls chant the best friends forever pack.

"Best friends forever ... We are friends till the end …. Let's share Our hopes, dreams, fears, and happy times …. Friends forever," Kalei repeats.

They reach up in the air , meeting mid-air for a high five. They shout in unison, "BFF's till the END!"

Kalei hears her mother calling from downstairs, and she responds. "Be right there, **makuahine.**"

"Kalei, what does makuahine mean?"

"It's my first language; we speak Hawaiian. It is a formal way to respect your mother, in my native language it means, Mother.

My family still speaks in our island language from time to time."

The girls rush downstairs upon arriving in the kitchen.

Mrs. Applegate directs the girls to the barstools in the eat-in kitchen. "Girls, we have something to talk to you about, will you take a seat?"

Willow fearfully looks at her mother; she stumbles to get out. "Is everything OK?" Miss Juno seems very pale, confused, and worried.

Mrs. Applegate, with a peaceful look, reaches out her hands to grab a hold of Kalei's hands.

Miss Applegate notices that Miss Juno is not reaching for Willow's hands. She is behaving like a dear staring in the headlights.

As, she turns to Miss Juno, glares at her, and whispers. "You know, being a glyphless one and all may be tough. I get that this may be hard to grasp or believe. But dear, let's shape up. Clara, you have to snap out of it, get with the program."

Mrs. Applegate turns her body back to the girls and grabs both of their hands. She tells them some folklore about the school of divination.

"You know, Kalei, do you remember the story that Kupuna Wahine would tell you about how you'll get your element one day?"

"Yes, ma'am. However, I don't remember much."

"Willow, Kalei has told me everything that happened at camp, from your levitation experience to riding with HydroKnox…. You're one of the chosen ones, Willow."

"Both of you girls need to understand you're coming of age; your 13th birthday will be over in the summer.

Your powers may come into full light a week before your birthday. Now listen closely; I will tell you a little about safety and the practice of magic."

Willow looks at Kalei, surprised. "Magic! Are you serious? The lady in the woods said this. Is this really true?"

"Yes Willow, this is for real, you both must understand it is a special gift to have magic; if you don't respect it (the almighty one can take it away), there are a few rules that I want you guys to memorize. Promise me never to use your skills to harm others."

"Yes, ma'am, we promise," said Willow.

"Yes Mom, I promise," said Kalei.

"Ok, these are the six golden rules every Wixan must follow. "The girls nod their heads to acknowledge what she says.

Sarah continues, " #1. Use your powers to help others, and never use them against free will.

#2. Honor the emerald tablets of knowledge; it is the holy grail of MANA Magic.

#3. Act as if you are a child of the Universe. Use the Laws of Attraction and meditate daily.

#4. Treat your own body as if it is a temple.

#5. Be kind and thoughtful and live with gratitude.

#6. Always… Always, believe in yourself, every day is a choice, to choose good over evil."

Both girls eagerly agree. "Yes, we understand, and we promise."

Mrs. Applegate comes from around the table; Miss Juno, no longer confused, follows suit with Mrs. Applegate. Both mothers embrace in a hug with their daughters.

Mrs. Applegate yells out. "GROUP HUG!" They all smile and give one big loving hug.

Later that night, at home, Willow goes to her mother. "Mum, I am having a hard time believing I am special….

 How can I be a chosen one? I'm just an ordinary girl born into an unloving world. Well Mom that was till I met you."

"Well, dear, extraordinary things happen to ordinary people. I may be a **glyphless** mom because I lack magical understanding and powers. But I believe in you." Clara embraces Willow in a loving hug.

As she caresses her hair with a gentleness. "Willow, you are the best kid; you are honest, smart, caring.

I also think you are the most outgoing daughter a mother could have ever wanted. I am beyond blessed to have you in my life, Willow.

So don't ever think you are unloved or unwanted. You are going to do great things with your life."

Willow feels the love in her mother's words and hugs her back, softly saying, "Mom, thank you for giving me this wonderful life with you and Aurora. You are an amazing mom."

Miss Juno sniffles, overwhelmed with emotion, as she senses the profound connection between her and the child, a gift from the divine. She recognizes Willow as a wondrous being entrusted to her care.

Understanding this, she resolves to allow Willow to flourish, embrace her innate magical potential, and share it with the world.

The next day, the girls make their way to the fridge for a drink. It's a cozy house on a Saturday afternoon.

Keanu and Chase are hiding in the kitchen with plastic jelly spiders, ready to prank Willow, Kalei, and Trinity, who are chatting in the living room.

Keanu whispers, "Chase these spiders look so real! Are you ready?"

Chase grinning ear to ear, "Totally! The girls are gonna freak out."

Keanu says, "Okay, let's go."

Keanu and Chase sneak into the living room, each holding a couple of plastic jelly spiders. They creep up behind the girls and suddenly throw the spiders on them.

Keanu shouts "Spiders!"

Willow screams, "Ahhh!... Get it off me!"

Kalei laughing nervously "Oh my, you two are total freakazoid's, I can't believe we are even related Keanu."

Trinity jumps up, "No way! Keep it away from me, its gross!"

Keanu and Chase start laughing and continue to chase the girls around the living room, holding the spiders out in front of them.

Chase teasing the girls. "Watch out, they're coming for you!"

Willow runs away yelling. "You guys are the worst!"

Kalei giggles, "Stop it, seriously"

Chase throws a few at her, Trinity dodges two spiders as she yells, "This isn't funny"

The girls run towards the kitchen, trying to escape the boys. As they dash through the doorway, they hit the saran wrap that Keanu and Chase had set up earlier.

Willow slams into the saran wrap, "What the—?"

The girls simultaneously fall into one another.

Keanu grabs the roll of packing scran wrap, then Chase grabs the other end of the wrap. Chase stands still holding it, as Keanu runs around the girls entrapping them.

"Keanu laughs and yells out, "Looks like you've got yourself wrapped up in a tight situation!"

Kalei laughs, "Oh no, we have been plasta~fied!"

Trinity pulls at the saran wrap" Help! We're stuck

Keanu is doubling over with laughter, he yells, "Gotcha! The spiders were just the beginning!"

Chase high-fives, Keanu, "Best prank ever!"

Willow laughs despite herself, "Okay… okay… you got us. Now help us get out of it."

Kalei still giggling, "Yeah, this was pretty clever."

Trinity looks at them smiling, "Just wait until we get you back!"

Keanu and Chase help the girls peel the saran wrap away, all of them laughing and chatting about the prank.

Keanu grins, "Don't get your big girl pants in a wad, it's all in good fun."

Chase smirks, "Yeah, but I think we're safe from revenge for a while, right?"

Willow playfully says, "Oh, we'll see about that."

Kalei with a mischievous look, "You'd better sleep with one eye open tonight. Revenge will be sweet."

Willow is laughing, "Yeah, you never know when we might strike back."

The break continues, and the next few days are filled with banter and camaraderie.

A few days before they leave for Hawaii. The girls are getting their foot lockers packed and their stuff ready for the exciting trip to the island.

The night before the trip to fly to the Island. Everyone gathers at Mr. and Mrs. Applegate's home for a bonfire and cookout. Everyone is there, Miss Juno, Willow, Mr. and Mrs. Applegate, Kalei, Keanu and his best friend Chase.

They all have a great time; Willow stays the night at Kalie's. Kalei sets Whizzy the Wizard's alarm to wake at 6 am. They all fall fast asleep, in anticipation of the exciting day tomorrow.

Whizzy the Alarm Wizard, rings loudly

"RING   RING   RING!

"My extraordinary magical ones! The sun is up, so it's time for you to rise and shine. It's a magical morning, and soon the adventures of the island await you!"

Kalei looks groggy, and responds, "Ugh… Whizzy, do you have to be so loud every morning?"

Whizzy the Alarm Wizard, with his hands on his hips, glares at her, "Of course, Kalei! How else would I ensure you make it to WillowBrook on time? The early magical ones catch the spell, after all!"

Willow stretches and yawns "He's got a point. We can't be late for our plane to the island. Thanks, Whizzy."

Trinity yawns and rubs her face to wake up, "Yeah! Yeah! But you don't have to be so cheerful about it? Morning are Hard! Whizzy!"

Whizzy the Alarm Wizard is always full of glee; a smile can be seen under his mustache that is moving rapidly as he talks. "Cheerful? Why not? ladies, a positive attitude is the best way to start a magical day! Besides, we've got quite the adventure ahead.

The adventures of the island, and a magnificent place called Manu`ahi summit. The summit isn't going to climb itself!"

Kalei says, "I suppose you're right. But what do you mean the Manu`ahi Summit, what is that?"

Whizzy says, "Not to worry when the time is right, you will know…. So, girls, let's get ready.

After your vacation on the island, you two have many adventures ahead. You'll have a Magic Banyan Tree to meet, the Manu`ahi Bird tonquer, and spells to learn."

Willow radiates a natural glow looking at her BFF, "Trinity, This is going to be phenomenal."

Whizzy with his caterpillar mustache moving rapidly, he says, "I heard that Professor Nightingale has some amazing new potions to teach you."

Willow with her eye raised, "Whizzy you know professors at the school? Who is Professor Nightingale?"

"Of course, Willow, I know more than it seems, you know I will leave you with a tidbit of information. Professor Nightengale is half Owl and half human, with a keen sense of sight."

Trinity "Plus, we can't forget about the other classes we'll have. What kind of magic will we get to learn?

Soon, we'll be at a real magic school! I'm so excited to meet the professors and all the new friends we'll make!"

Whizzy replies, "That's the spirit! But just remember it's not official until you receive a delivery of your commencement letter. Remember, magic is in the air, and every step you take brings you closer to your dreams. Now, let's get moving! Time waits for no witch!"

Kalei snarkily says, "Alright, alright Whizzy, lead the way with that boundless energy of yours."

Whizzy smiles and points to the door, "Onward, to Oahu, Hawaii. Where your Extraordinary Destiny begins!

The path is paved with wonders, and WillowBrook School of Magic awaits its brightest witches!"

Willow smiles, "Thanks, Whizzy. We're lucky to have you waking us up every morning."

Trinity grabs Whizzy and places him in his travel carrier. She looks more positive, "Yeah, you may be loud, but you make it hard not to smile. Let's marvel at this day!"

Now fully awake and excited, the girls take their footlockers and belongings to the car. Mrs. and Mr. Applegate, Keanu, Willow, and Trinity get loaded into the vehicle.

They set off toward Orlando International Airport, their spirits are high and ready for the self-discovering, spirit-enriching, and magical days ahead.

CHARACTERS

Billy Baxter, School Bully.

Miss Juno (Clara Juno), is Willow's adoptive mother.

Fran,   Operation Snowball Cabin Mate

Federico Barcelona, is a foreign exchange student from Spain, at a pie-eating contest at the New Horizon School.

Gabriella, The Lady in the Woods.

HydroKnox, Kalei's water Protector.

Johnny, the boy nearly drowns at camp.

Judy, The pet caretaker at the Humane Society shelter.

Kalei Applegate is Willow's best friend. She was born on the Hawaiian island of Lanai.

Keanu Applegate is Kalei's brother. He was born in Oahu, North Kohala (Now lives in Florida).

Miss Shoemaker, Meditation Leader.

Mr. Steven Applegate, Kalei's father.

Mr. Kouts, is Kalei's favorite gym teacher.

Mr. Sanchez,   Pottery and Arts teacher &

Pie eating contest announcer.

Mrs. Applegate, Kalei's Mother.

Mrs. Runkle's, 5th period, Kalei's teacher.

Mrs. Sandalwood, Willow's favorite teacher

Miss Shoemaker, Camp Meditation leader.

Mrs. Simmons, Camp counselor and leader of the meditation group.

Trinity Wolf, Willow, and Kalei's friend. Trinity Wolf was born in Georgia; she is a Cherokee Nation citizen. Trinity is taller than most, teens her age. Often, she wears her hair in braided pigtails, her hair is a dark brownish black.

Willow Juno, Kalei's BFF. Born in Largo Florida, Left at the hospital, unwanted by her mother. She grew up in the Florida foster care system till she was 12. Origin and background are unknown.

Zeda, Operation Snowball Cabin Mate.

WB ~~ Enchantments

Departure No Low Aires: Vanishes into thin air.

Firemortus: To create fire from the palm of the hand.

Language Reference:

Hawaiian Language

1. **Aloha** (ah-loh-hah) — Love, compassion, or a friendly greeting, used to say hello or goodbye.

2. **Aloha wau iā 'oe** (ah-loh-hah vow ee-ah oh-eh) — I love you.

3. **'Anakē** (ah-nah-keh) — Auntie.

4. **Tūtū wahine** (too-too wah-hee-neh) — Grandmother.

5. **Hoaloha** (hoh-ah-loh-hah) — Friend.

6. **Keanu** (keh-ah-noo) — A boy's name meaning "cool breeze."

7. **Keiki** (kay-kee) — Child.

8. **Kupuna kāne** (koo-poo-nah kah-neh) — Grandfather.

9. **Kupuna wahine** (koo-poo-nah wah-hee-neh) — Grandmother.

10. **Makua** (mah-koo-ah) — Parent.

11. **Makua kāne** (mah-koo-ah kah-neh) — Father.

12. **Makuahine** (mah-koo-ah-hee-neh) — Mother.

13. **Mahalo** (mah-hah-loh) — Thank you.

14. Pūʻuwai (poo-oo-vai) — Best friend (translates to "heart" or "soul," often implying a deep emotional connection).

15. Pūliki (poo-lee-kee) — Hug.

16. Tūtū (too-too) — Grandmother or Elder.

17. ʻOhana (oh-hah-nah) — Family.

♪ ♫ ♪ About the Author ♫♪♫

I Choose Joy.

Reach ~ Love ~ Impact

DC Daniel is an author whose profound life experiences have deeply shaped their writing journey. Growing up as an unwanted child in foster care and enduring a challenging upbringing, they found the inspiration to create ☽ The Magic of WillowBrook ✤ —a series that empowers young readers facing adversity on their path to adulthood.

Their creation, the WillowBrook Series, is a testament to their ability to transport readers into enchanting worlds while addressing real-life struggles with sensitivity and empathy. With a deep understanding of the challenges young people face, DC Daniel weaves captivating children's novels that blend imaginative storytelling with themes of resilience and triumph over hardship.

LOVE NOTES:

Every one of you, out there in the world, unplug from the matrix and discover life. Take a deep breath in and know everything will work out in the end.

SENDING LOVE ~ LIGHT ~ POSITIVE ENERGY

"May rays of inspiration and light guide you through the ugly, mean, and challenging parts of life. Furthermore; in your journey, may you find strength, wisdom, and grace to transform every obstacle into a stepping stone, to get where you want to go in life."

Here is *Desiderata*, the beloved poem.

Desiderata is a prose poem written by American author Max Ehrmann in 1927. The title comes from the Latin phrase desiderata, which means "things desired"

Desiderata

Go placidly amid the noise and haste,

and remember what peace there may be in silence.

As far as possible, without surrender,

be on good terms with all persons.

Speak your truth quietly and clearly;

and listen to others,

even to the dull and the ignorant;

they too have their story.

Avoid loud and aggressive persons,

they are vexatious to the spirit.

If you compare yourself with others,

you may become vain or bitter,

for always there will be greater and lesser persons than

DC Daniel

yourself.

Enjoy your achievements as well as your plans.

Keep interested in your own career, however humble;

it is a real possession in the changing fortunes of time.

Exercise caution in your business affairs,

for the world is full of trickery.

But let this not blind you to what virtue there is;

many persons strive for high ideals,

and everywhere life is full of heroism.

Be yourself.

Especially, do not feign affection.

Neither be cynical about love;

for in the face of all aridity and disenchantment

it is as perennial as the grass.

Take kindly the counsel of the years,

gracefully surrendering the things of youth.

Nurture strength of spirit

to shield you in sudden misfortune.

But do not distress yourself with dark imaginings.

Many fears are born of fatigue and loneliness.

Beyond a wholesome discipline,

be gentle with yourself.

You are a child of the universe

no less than the trees and the stars;

you have a right to be here.

And whether or not it is clear to you,

no doubt the universe is unfolding as it should.

Therefore, be at peace with God,

whatever you conceive Him to be,

and whatever your labors and aspirations,

in the noisy confusion of life keep peace with your soul.

With all its sham, drudgery, and broken dreams,

it is still a beautiful world.

Be cheerful.

Strive to be happy.

~~~~~~

~ Be kind to yourself, unplug from the Matrix and digital life. Go outside, go to the forest, experience life, read a book, and learn something new every day. ~ DC Daniel

~~~~~~

~ This book is dedicated to all the kids in the world who struggle, every day, with fitting in, self-acceptance, self-esteem, self-worth, and finding their unique path in life.

~   You are not alone in your journey, and this dedication is a tribute to your strength, resilience, and the incredible potential within each one of you.

~   May this book serve as a source of inspiration and comfort as you navigate the challenges of growing up and discovering your true selves.

~   Remember, your uniqueness is your superpower, and the world is a better place with your one-of-a-kind contributions.

~   Keep believing in yourself, keep striving for your dreams, and never forget that you are loved, valued, and capable of achieving greatness in your wheelhouse, no matter the adversity and hardships you have faced in life. Just keep swimming and never give up.

~   When finding your way, find your voice. You are the heroes of your own stories, facing challenges with courage and resilience.

~   Remember, you are never alone, and your uniqueness is your greatest strength. May this book be a beacon of hope, reminding you that you are valued, cherished, and capable of achieving incredible things.

✦ Note from Author ✦

For all the young readers and aspiring Magical Wixans, embracing this journey is a true privilege. I want you to know that the challenges you face as a child are very real, and like me, you will emerge victorious as you step into adulthood. Hold onto the essence of Mana within your heart, and guard against the encroachment of Spector, ensuring it never dims your inner light.

REMEMBER THESE

QUOTES FOR LIFE

Life is 10 % what happens to us and 90 % how we react to it." ~ Charles R. Swindoll

"Success is not final; failure is not fatal: It is the courage to continue, that counts." ~ Winston Churchill

"Believe you can and you're halfway there." ~ Theodore Roosevelt

"The greatest glory in living lies not in never falling, but in rising every time we fall." ~ Nelson Mandela

"You are never too small to make a difference." ~ Greta Thunberg

"You are braver than you believe, stronger than you seem, and smarter than you think." ~ A.A. Milne (from Winnie the Pooh)

The pessimist complains about the wind. The optimist expects it to change. The leader adjusts the sails and picks up the pace. ~DC Daniel

"Your current situation is not your final destination." ~DC Daniel

Let your smile change the world, but don't let the world change your smile. ~Unknown

Just keep swimming. ~DC Daniel

"Keep your Mana shining bright, and never stop believing in the power of your dreams and vibrations." ~DC Daniel

"The laws of attraction are powerful: you attract what you say, what you do, and what you dream. Ultimately, you attract what you permit into your life. ~DC Daniel

These next 8 blank pages are for you, to dream, draw, doodle, write or do, and complete your reality and destiny. WBOME body with a League of Extraordinary Humans.

Mystic Tides

DC Daniel

☆ Mystic Tides ☾

DC Daniel

Keep Swimming ~ Keep Striving to be your best

The poem on the next page is for you to tear out and
hang somewhere.

Desiderata

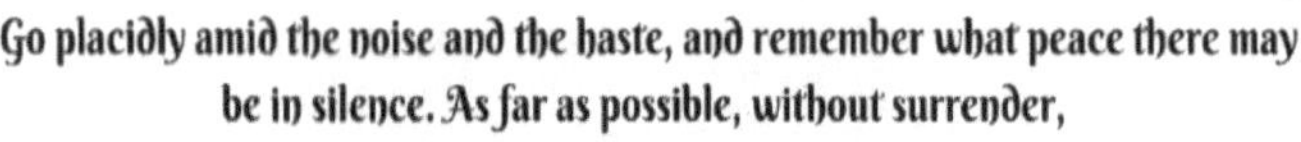

Go placidly amid the noise and the haste, and remember what peace there may
be in silence. As far as possible, without surrender,
be on good terms with all persons.
Speak your truth quietly and clearly; and listen to others, even to the dull
and the ignorant; they too have their story.
Avoid loud and aggressive persons; they are vexatious to the spirit. If you
compare yourself with others, you may become vain or bitter, for always
there will be greater and lesser persons than yourself.
Enjoy your achievements as well as your plans. Keep interested in your own
career, however humble; it is a real possession in the changing fortunes of time.
Exercise caution in your business affairs, for the world is full of trickery.
But let this not blind you to what virtue there is; many persons strive for
high ideals, and everywhere life is full of heroism.
Be yourself. Especially do not feign affection. Neither be cynical about love; for
in the face of all aridity and disenchantment, it is as perennial as the grass.
Take kindly the counsel of the years, gracefully surrendering the things of youth.
Nurture strength of spirit to shield you in sudden misfortune. But do not distress
yourself with dark imaginings. Many fears are born of fatigue and loneliness.
Beyond a wholesome discipline, be gentle with yourself. You are a child of
the universe no less than the trees and the stars; you have a right to be here.
And whether or not it is clear to you, no doubt the universe is unfolding as it
should. Therefore be at peace with God, whatever you conceive Him to be.
And whatever your labors and aspirations, in the noisy confusion of life,
keep peace in your soul. With all its sham, drudgery and broken dreams, it is
still a beautiful world. Be cheerful. Strive to be happy.

by Max Ehrmann ©1927